Good As News

A Playful Exploration
Of The Human Condition
Via Short Story Musings
On Events And Things

by Alain Brunet

Coffee Break Long

Short Thoughtful Stories

'Good As News' repairs events

and things 'good as new'

Family-album-style lets you imagine each picture
viewed from your perspective as the story quickly
frames details for your enjoyment.

Cover picture information:

North view from the deck after an overnight escape in the
cozy inn of the restored Brandy Pot Lighthouse in the
middle of the St. Lawrence River in September 2017

Title: Good As News

© Alain Brunet 2017 – Copyright Canada 1143823

Legal Deposit:
Bibliothèque et Archives nationales du Québec, 2018.

Author and Editor: Alain Brunet
Published using: Amazon Kindle Direct Publishing
Available as Paperback or eBook on www.amazon.com

ISBN : 978-0-9953280-1-3 (printed book)
ISBN : 978-0-9953280-2-0 (eBook)

Introduction to **Good As News**

May this book be inviting enough to have you sit in the chair with a view and read one or many of these 100 reality based stories, each one short enough to fit in a coffee break.

I wrote them from 2015 to 2017 in Quebec and Florida hoping to make your imagination smile. In the process, experiences were refurbished and embellished to render them Good as New. Concepts are formatted as Good as News bulletins.

Being mindful of possibly losing my cursive handwriting ability is what prompted me to begin writing. Newly retired from the obligations of a day job, occasions to write were becoming fewer. I have never kept a diary and have no intention of starting. Nonetheless, not feeling ready to write stories at that point, I started writing what happened the previous day. This also exercised my short term memory.

In a standard size school notebook I filled a page this way every morning while eating breakfast. After writing yesterday's date at the top, I numbered each page and filled it with about 300 words. Some days' mindset allowed me to be a little creative and helped me persevere for 1,000 days without skipping a single one.

As I saw the one-thousandth day coming, I built up my courage and decided to write fiction before I got totally bored with yesterday's accounts. At first I used pictures and images on placemats and magazines to imagine stories as if I had been there when they were created. Over time, people I met and places I visited gave me ample topics and helped me remain more 'cursively' abled.

Please note that any resemblance to reality is totally coincidental to the desire for a better world.

Stone Age

In the middle of Stone Age lived a big strong man called Fred. His ancestors mostly resided in caves but Fred was tired of living in a hole and preferred to build a ground-level structure allowing fresh air to breeze through. His friends did not see how it could be done so they remained in isolated areas where you may find hills possibly with caves. Already as a child, Fred had played with stones, carving them to various shapes. Now fully grown up, he used his considerable strength and rolled them to whatever location he liked. Wanting to set his house on an ideal site, he chose to be close to a lake but far enough so that the spring thaw would not affect him. This area is now just south of the corner of Westchester and Devon Streets in Bedrock, Quebec.

Fred found that another advantage to this site was the fact that the ground was loaded with stones of various shapes and sizes. Lily had a green thumb and was known to be able to grow a multitude of vegetables, herbs and fruits. When she saw Fred's efforts to build a home, she offered to help him and decided to stay with him instead of following her tribe as nomads. As Fred removed stones from the ground, Lily leveled an area and made it into a lovely garden.

Their home had two rooms of about 12 x 12 feet. One was their bedroom and the other the kitchen. The stone fireplace was positioned in the center and heated both rooms in the winter. Bedrock was woodsy back then as now with cedar trees, so he used them to make the roof and their bed. With a clear view to the east and the west, they enjoyed wonderful sunrise and sunset from their kitchen table. Cedar edges shielded the north side from chilly winds while the south side was clear enough to provide ample light to their living quarters. Soon, friends marveled at these amenities and started moving out of dark and humid caves to more houses built by Fred. Bedrock became famous for this trail lined with lovely chipped stone houses, all facing south with a view on the lake. Westchester Street is the current name of this trail still on the same panoramic ridge.

Not much else is left today from that era except for a sleek rounded stone in our garden. If you look closely on it, you will see Fred's ear engraved in it since he was probably using it as a pillow and peacefully died in his sleep.

Djavar

His morning started just like any normal work day. As usual at 6:30am, Eddy was already on Highway 20 driving in heavy traffic. On the radio, traffic man announced an accident and a traffic jam getting worse by the minute where Eddy was heading. Knowing the area very well, he left the highway through the next exit, like some other drivers. Luckily not many went his way along Donegani and other small streets. He was moving well and even with the many stops and traffic lights, he still had a chance of arriving on time at the office.

Thirty employees were expected to be present that morning for the monthly review meeting led by Eddy. While he was waiting at a red light on Papineau, he was thinking about his opening remarks when a violent impact hit his car on the passenger side and he got sprayed by glass debris. His car, pushed sideways, ended up crushed against a corner building. His head banged his side glass so hard that the window broke and he blacked-out. The truck driver who rammed him was driving through his green light at about 50 km/hr when he steered left to avoid four pedestrians. The four teenagers were chasing each other for fun on their way to school and suddenly showed-up in front of his truck. Remorse got them to run and pull Eddy out of his car because a strong odor of gas was coming from the area. They were only ten meters away when the two vehicles burst into flames. Eddy's car had broken a gas valve on the outside wall of the building. It now fed the fire enough to incinerate both his car and the truck.

A week went by and Eddy was still in the intensive care unit at the hospital. He had left home so quickly that he had thrown his wallet into his briefcase. His face and hands were so covered in bandages that it took days to confirm his ID. His wallet and briefcase had burned with his car. His wife, friends and colleagues had reported him missing. Authorities took a few days to link this unidentified injured man to the one reported missing. When they were allowed to visit him, they were all really worried when he did not recognize anybody.

Today was the first day he spoke again but it was obvious that he suffers from amnesia. Djavar was the one who gave everyone hope. When Eddy had left home on the fatal morning, Djavar had given him a big lick on his ear and side of his face while he was picking-up his briefcase. Finally, Eddy was released from the hospital and allowed to go home. That same night, Djavar managed to give him another good lick on the ear. And, that is when Eddy's memory returned.

Phone

None of this may have happened if they had left on time. He was waiting for her in the car but after ten minutes he came back in to see what was holding her. She was on the phone and waved at him to stay quiet so she could hear. As she was going to turn on the alarm and walk out, the phone rang so she had rushed to get it. Her godfather is now 85 and still lives in a large cottage close to Portland, Maine. They used to see each other often but for the last twenty years or so, they would only speak on the phone twice a year for their individual birthday. Now at age 60, like her husband, they had just retired and did not have children.

Godfather lived alone almost as a hermit after losing his wife and two kids in a plane crash 28 years ago. He came close to re-marrying two times but it fell through, so he decided to live alone and use only the main floor of his two storey house facing the Atlantic. He can spend days in his solarium and not be bored, just watching waves breaking on the rocky coastline. He rarely misses the magic of the sun rising out of the ocean. People come to help him and to maintain the house but now he decided he would phone all his relatives because his doctor told him cancer may take him within a year. She was the first that godfather phoned out of a list of fifteen other relatives that he liked.

His health was getting worse by the day and the doctor said it was unsafe for him and neighbors if he stayed alone. So he needed staff or family to live with him otherwise they were ordering him to move to a nursing home. He tried staff but they had to change often because he did not like them. That is when he phoned his 60 year old godchild. He invited her and her husband to come and live with him for a while. Remembering how beautiful the scenery and the house were, they decided to give it a try. Godfather died nine months later but they shared marvelous quality time with him. He gave them the house in his will and they elected to live there forever, always glad to answer the phone, just in case.

WordsCastle

They are only words but teamed up as they are, they represent a kingdom for humanity. They hang out just a short walk away from my home. What a lovely stroll it is to dive into them while visiting our local public library. Located just across the street from Lac St-Louis, I always struggle to decide if I will stretch my legs by the lake or tickle my brain in the words castle.

Last night the weather was pristine and mild so, I blended a bit of both. Sailboats mooring in the bay all had twins, mirrored in the perfectly flat water. A few geese looked like remote controlled crafts, scanning the surroundings and enjoying the scenery. Before it was too late, I entered the Library, welcomed by friendly volunteers, one of them handled the book I returned and we were both reassured when the computer confirmed the transaction by the "return" virtual voice message. With an hour or so to spare before closing, my magical mystery tour started.

The novelties display got my attention first. Then I browsed the magazine section. Attracted by the TV sets review on the Consumers' Report, I decided to sit and read it. Comfortably settled with a view of the lake, one can only marvel at how lucky we are. Friends and neighbours stopped by to say hello. But we all respect our individual venture in this paradise so we keep our voice down and conversation short. A lot of my favourite authors come from random discovery. So I like to wander into the sections and read the back cover of a few books. Like a magnet, a book will draw my eyes. Samuel De Champlain is one of my encounters. Remembering him as an explorer that came from France to found Quebec City in 1608, I wondered why someone would write a book of 834 pages about him. David Hackett Fisher, an acclaimed historian of Baltimore was probably fascinated by the numerous exploits of Champlain. And I am sure they would both gladly come to explore with us our wonderful Lakeshore WordsCastle.

Artichoke

Nestled in a wonderful valley of southern Italy, the vegetable garden of Lorenzo was already providing a lot of the small family's needs. To show it to his friends in Canada, he used the old table in the garden shed to take a picture. Nicely laid out on the table and in a basket, he had onions, tomatoes, garlic, sunflower, red peppers and artichokes. A beautiful array of flowers also from his garden provided a colourful background.

Arturo, Lorenzo's brother went to Canada as a teenager playing soccer and elected to go back to live there. Maria, a lovely cheerleader for the home team in St-Leonard, Quebec had a big crush for Arturo. Her father was an old friend of Arturo's father and both were very happy when their children got married at 20 years old. Arturo who always enjoyed cooking, now 55 years old, he opened a small Pizzeria in Dorval and named it Gigi, in honour of his mother's name.

They live in a small town called Beaurepaire and, Maria having been an executive administrator for 20 years with Bell Canada, decided to put her skills to use for her community and became Mayor. Having visited Lorenzo many times in Italy, they both could remember the multitude of fragrances and peaceful scenery of this paradise valley. Arturo succeeded in reproducing some of that feeling in his pizzeria. He has a lot of success with his thin crust pizza with garlic, olive oil, mozzarella cheese, basil and artichoke all wisely spread over his special tomato paste that he makes himself using dried tomatoes he gets from Lorenzo's garden.

Pacha

Pacha the Cat is very busy. As soon as he hears someone walking through the house, he rushes to the winter (insulated) solarium and stands by the door. Being a well behaved cat, he will wait by the door so that someone will open it for him. After about two minutes of waiting, he will meow repeatedly to be sure we have noticed his desire. Once out that door, in the summer (screened only) solarium, Lorraine sets him up comfortably with a cushion on a chair but she never lets him go outside. Pacha does not care for this now. He must first inspect the area. This summer solarium is almost at ground level, with only screens between him and the outside.

Sniffing all his boundaries, he figures who has visited during the night. So far he has detected squirrels, cats, skunks, birds and raccoons. If no other animal has noticed his arrival, he will sing long meows that can be heard three houses away. Pruneau, the other cat that lives with Lorraine, will be the first to show up and join Pacha, but just outside the screen because he sleeps out of doors. Pruneau now sits by the house, anxious to come-in and be fed. Squirrels come to play in the big maple tree close to Pacha who likes watching them run around the trunk at amazing speed. Once Pruneau comes in, Pacha tries to hypnotize birds that walk on the lawn picking amazingly long worms. Pacha's big eyes seem to fascinate some of the birds that stare back at him, probably wondering why he stares so much.

But then, it is Pruneau who stands by the door, eager to go back out. As soon as he steps out of the house he runs after the birds. Hiding under the cedar edge, he keeps a close watch on them but, often falls asleep in the shade. After watching all this excitement, Pacha walks back inside for his 10 to noon shift in the living room window. From this vantage lookout position, he sees all neighbors walking their dogs or, Sylvie and Lorraine working in the flower garden or playing with Pruneau. Soon we notice that Pacha is asleep and blending all this in probably magnificent dreams because we often see him smile in his sleep.

Power Walker

Taking it for a walk on a sunny afternoon is almost enjoyable. Our usual outing lasts about an hour and is a good workout. The uneven terrain caused by roots of five large maple trees requires good ankles capable of constant flexing. To keep up with it you must maintain a pace of about 5 km/h and under the sun you easily build-up a sweat.

Having played tennis for three hours the morning of the same day, I had lunch with my wife on our patio and we enjoyed this quality time together. I always wait to go for this walk in the afternoon, this way the ground is dryer and I do not get my feet wet from walking in the morning dew. I also wear safety sun glasses to protect my eyes from blowing dust and nasty UVs. Looks like my activities have inspired my neighbors to also get moving. The one in front across the street is now in a wheelchair and was out with a friend checking his house. Our south side neighbor was also out walking but she was going in a north-south direction while I was mostly going east-west.

It is also a pleasant way to meet acquaintances like Janet, a town councillor, who was walking back home from the Sailing Club, just down our street. Also the town Mayor honked her horn and waved when she drove by me. Once I am done, I always go back to pick up the remaining excess trash and use a hand operated clipper to trim around trees. Power Walker is what I call it because it has handles just like the walker that seniors use to keep their balance while walking, but mine is self-propelled at 5 km/h and will drag you along if you keep your grip on the handle. This is probably why the gas tank in my Craftsman Lawnmower can make it run for only 90 minutes so it will not drag me too far if I fall but still hang on to it.

Mud Room

The Mud Room in this house is the busiest part of it. Quiet for now but it is the entrance used most of the time.   Located on the side of the house, it is conveniently close to the car parking area and provides easy access to the kitchen when carrying groceries.   Kids spend hours there on the window bench to watch birds coming to the feeder just outside.   Mary is very proud of the lantern that her husband John installed in the entry way. They bought it in a flea market, all rusted but the glass reflectors were still good.   After changing the socket and wiring, it was good as new. Removing the rust was a challenge and required a lot of elbow juice but, the end result with its black glossy finish looks great.

Except for winter months, the rubber boots are always on the shoe rack, ready along with the basket, to go mushroom picking. This is how Mary and John met while attending a wild mushroom identification class. Adjusting to the weather, they always find a day every week to look for mushrooms in the woods close to their house and use this quality time together to chat. Now fairly experienced at it, they rarely need to buy mushrooms at the grocery store.

Returning home, using the mirror on the Mud Room wall brings another load of souvenirs. Ten years ago when they bought the house, they found an old wine barrel in the shed. John salvaged a ring of solid oak and got a mirror cut to fit it. The wood is cleaned but John purposely left some aging marks on it to give it more rusticity. With the windows opened you feel the breeze through the lovely screened door. It is almost sad to leave this casual vestibule and step into the other rooms just as exquisite but much more formal.

Daylight

Having the time to appreciate the magic of a sunny morning is a privilege that enchants me every time. Numerous shades of green in the foliage are emphasized by the shape and size of leaves. Birds celebrate the new day by singing to one another and digging long worms out of the lawn. A rabbit, not sure if it is always the same one, crosses our backyard on its way to visit neighbourhood lots. Often cats follow a similar path. One can wonder if the cat follows the rabbit or is it the other way around.

Then the wind comes into play. Trees start dancing, moved by invisible waves but maintaining harmony. Clouds follow that flow, mixing their various shades of grey and white to the light blue background of the sky. Big birds glide through them, waving their wings to salute the new day. After a good night of sleep, squirrels look like they are fully cranked-up as they race after one another around tree trunks and often jump from tree to tree. A fully white squirrel showed up today and was an amazing contrast to the pitch black one with it.

All above is transformed suddenly and for many morning hours. When daylight shows up, every minute offers a different display. Shades move along and add mystery with strange forms that appear on trees and every object in its way. Many flowers open up to show-off after spending the night all wrapped up. This blooming of new energy has such a beneficial effect on us also that we always make sure to get a full load of daylight every morning while we eat breakfast.

MacDonald

On her way to San Jose (or anywhere else, it is just that it rhymes well) Mary stopped every two hours on average, to stretch her legs. So far a rest area had shown up sporadically to match this schedule. But now, the next one was another hour away and she needed to get gas so, she took the next exit with services. A small sign read 'Welcome to Jerome population 238 and growing'. The exit road led to a beautiful valley of farmland surrounded by rolling hills. Located about a mile off the highway, the service station was part of a dozen small buildings. Everywhere else was crops.

As she drove closer, she first thought she had vision problems but sure enough, the gas pumps were under a porch in front of the church. Three of the four pumps were in use, so she drove up to the fourth one. At the same time she saw a smiling young woman walk to her car. While Mary was opening her car door to do the refill, the woman introduced herself and said she would gladly fill-up, check the oil and windshield washer liquid so that Mary could walk around or use the restrooms. Seeing other customers with children and mostly friendly faces around, she went into the church.

The vestibule was fairly large and housed an information desk busy with people. She read signs giving the history of Jerome. This village had died and the last residents had moved out 20 years ago. John MacDonald who owns fast food restaurants all over the world, decided to buy it all and retire here. This farmland valley now supplies some of his new veggie menu needs and every day, people stop here for gas, some never leave. Often they join the town choir or play one of the many music instruments, free to use in the church. Being an unemployed industrial designer going to look for work in San Jose, she could not believe her luck and accepted, on the spot, the open position to help design new signs and packaging for John. Why not stay in Jerome since she did not know where else she was going, any more than I do?

Happy Waves

It started on the day after moving into their new house, a sense of well-being Diane and René had never felt before. Sure enough the house was the cause. As soon as they left for work that feeling was gone. The house has been built in 1955 and needed renovations. The two restrooms were stripped to the studs and new plumbing along with all new apparatus were installed in a more modern design. Then they had the house re-painted with pleasant colours that emphasized their furniture. Luckily the mysterious happy feeling remained.

Determined to find what caused this happiness and protect it, they went up into the attic and inspected every corner using a powerful search light. All was in order above so they looked below. The basement had water damage when the sump pump failed many years ago. The former owners had fixed it and installed a new carpet but the distinctive smell of mildew persisted. So they removed the carpet and the plywood floor under it to get to the concrete floor. It was covered by old vinyl tiles which smell of mildew. All of it was scraped off and the concrete floor and walls were disinfected before a new wood floor was installed.

The good feeling remained but they were always worried about losing it every time they changed something in the house. Replacing the windows and the front door was their main fear. This was now essential because the old ones kept the house cold and hard to heat during winter months. After all these renovations they invited friends over and they all felt it too. Strangely the solution to this mystery came to René on June 25th. When he went camping with his brother for a few days, he could not believe it when the next morning, he got that same feeling. As he unzipped the door of his tent and noticed he was at ground level, the feeling hit him like a wave. So now they know that this extra feeling of happiness comes from the fact that the main floor of their house is only one foot above ground and gives them loads of happy ground waves.

Fondness

Believe it or not, they have never met. Yet they live on the same street, with only five houses between them. My two friends have lived in this location for over twenty years and each raised a family. These are great people that I like a lot but they do not attend local social events and I must respect the fact that they are not as ready as I am to make new friends. Over the years I am sure they have seen each other while going for a walk or at the grocery store but never took the extra step to officially meet.

My wife does not like social events either and like my friends, I know it is useless to try to change someone over 60 years old that is set in his ways. Luckily my town offers a lot of activities that fit my interest to meet people. The main one for me is the tennis club and its 400 members. I do not know them all but I surely have a fun relationship with over 100 of them. They come from so many various origins that being with them is like travelling all over the world. Even almost better considering that when you travel abroad, you get very little chance to meet the same people long enough to have in depth discussions with them. Take this 63 years old man I met last week to play tennis with him for the first time. He came from Romania with the Rugby team for the Montreal 1976 Olympics and never left. We had a pleasant conversation and he assured me that he had travelled all over the world and that our town is the best place to be.

No wonder most of the people I meet here look happy. So I challenge the notion and meet more people at the library, at city hall, at the dog park or just walking. My new project is to meet all neighbors that live up to three houses away from us. At least by phone to start and hopefully to meet them officially. This way I will rest assured that my surroundings are safe and that we are all keeping a mutual fondness.

Politics

Amazingly enough, some people with great minds and abilities elect to no longer get involved in their community after retiring. Often due to bad health, they must restrict themselves to petting animals, reading, cooking and walking. Some lucky others who still feel strong and healthy, fear boredom and seek activities. Often they have attained top management level at work and cannot stop thriving with a loaded agenda every day. So they get involved in clubs, in committees, even in politics.

That is what is happening to Gilbert. He sold his company a few years ago and retired with a good pension plan and a few millions. After a few cruises and trips in remote areas of the world, he was invited to join a friend and become a candidate in the current Canadian Federal Election. A little worried by his high blood pressure, his doctor assured him that he could go for it if he took a pill every morning. His party was already leading but got a boost from his candidacy. All his public meetings were well attended while he enjoyed making the most of his charismatic and public speaking abilities. Trading ideas with the party leader, they proposed an important new project for Canada.

Like most countries, Canada started along the shores of waterways. So the main cities are along the coast of the Atlantic and Pacific Oceans, the Saint-Lawrence River and the Great Lakes. What really got the Canadian economy growing was when the railway was built from East to West, linking all the cities. Now that they have become densely populated, railroads are filled to capacity and space is not available to add more rails. Gilbert proposed a new railroad going straight from central Canada to the Gulf of Saint-Lawrence along the 50th parallel. Built at least 15km away from any populated area, safe from possible disasters and noise, Canada exports can go faster and safer to the Atlantic Ocean, helping the Canadian economy.

Even central states of the USA see the new railroad as the most efficient way to avoid going over the Rocky Mountains or through the heavily populated areas of the east coast. Wood, oil, ore and any other bulk freight can now be shipped efficiently to export markets. Existing tracks can now be dedicated to supplying cities that attracted them in the first place. Commuter and other passenger trains will less be delayed by shipments abroad.

This project may never be built or take twenty years to become reality but it is a great enough challenge to maintain Gilbert's eagerness to stay in the swing of things.

Brunswick

The fact that we have always lived far from the ocean gives it that much more charm when we go to see it. We live in the greater Montreal, Quebec area and the most popular ocean destination is also the closest, at a six hours' driving distance. The too familiar 'No Vacancy' sign is lit on most motels in the summer as they quickly all get packed with Quebecers. Old Orchard Beach, Maine is the summer home for many Eastern Canadian families, so much that a few now own a motel and became American citizens.

We got married on Canadian Thanksgiving Day, which falls on the second Monday in October. Most years we would stretch the long weekend by a few days and go on a small trip. Walking on a wide and long sandy beach is our favorite relaxing activity. We had never stayed at Old Orchard Beach as kids mainly because our families could not afford it. Now that we could, we once brought my wife's parents with us and stayed in a huge two-storey penthouse condo. It had twenty-five feet wide of windows overlooking the Atlantic Ocean. We liked this old six-storey building called the Brunswick so much that we have been back to stay there more than ten times. It's located directly on the beach and waking up in our top-floor bedroom, we could literally watch from our bed, the sun, majestically rising out of the ocean.

In mid-October, Old Orchard Beach is like a ghost town. A lot of summer houses and motels are closed and boarded up for winter. But the beach remains magnificent and around noon, it is often warm enough to walk barefoot on the sand. It is about three miles long, only limited by a river at both ends and, halfway there is a pier that we walk under. Fishermen are very active off the coast of Maine and they have a co-op store in Old Orchard Beach from which we can buy fresh lobster every day. Within thirty minutes' drive either way, we can also visit interesting sites like Portland or Ogunquit. Long live the Brunswick because we have visited many other beach resorts but never found one in a more beautiful and peaceful setting to celebrate our wedding anniversary.

Why Not?

It was nearly over before it started. Maggie had played a lot of tennis as a teenager and in her twenties but only a few times a year since. Like most housewives of her era, she had devoted all her time and energy to her husband, her children and to her career. Now in her sixties, she lives alone in a small apartment in Pointe-Claire. That is where she moved after selling their family house. It has already been fifteen years since Bob, her husband, died from a heart attack. The four bedroom house was way too big for her alone. Her daughter and two sons had moved far away either to follow a spouse or work or both. She elected to free herself from running the big empty house.

Having worked as a Cosmetic Beauty Advisor at Fairview Shopping Center for thirty five years, she retired three years ago and loved every minute of her new life. Maggie's apartment building was close enough to the village and she enjoyed walking there every day when the weather was pleasant. She was also only a block away from the Clearpoint Tennis Club. Many of her friends had asked her to join for many years and she finally did. Now part of a group of retired women, she plays almost every weekday mornings and joins the Saturday Round Robin and BBQ to mingle with other club members and guests.

At the last annual general meeting, Maggie accepted her nomination to manage the Club's publicity. She enjoys the company of all eight members of the management committee so she considers their meetings as another interesting social event. The committee meeting of this week was the first one of the new year and in preparation for the next season. Still they found time to share Christmas family gathering stories and plans for the balance of winter. The meeting was about to end when George openly invited Maggie to join him and spend the next three months in his beach-front condo in Florida. They know each other well by now and have been on a few weekend trips together. Everyone around the table looked surprised but all encouraged Maggie to live it up and she joyfully replied Why Not?

Yours

"A bird in hand is worth two in the bush". Gary was asking me for my advice and I used the above saying for guidance. He is considering changing jobs but cannot afford to go the wrong way. Now married to Julia for ten years, they have a six years old son and live in a nice cottage in Laval. Julia works for the government and their combined income is essential to cover the mortgage on their house. Gary is an electronics engineer, responsible for a group of twenty-five employees in a large corporation.

Dependant on contracts and projects all over the world, Gary was sent by his employer to lead other teams on site in very far countries. Some of the trips his wife could go along but most of them he was alone for a few months. The current unstable global economy and profits driven shareholders, spread the rumors of massive layoffs in Gary's company. If he waits for his job to be terminated, he will be amongst hundreds all looking for a job and reduce his chances. Even if he stayed, he does not want to work in other countries anymore.

For years Gary has been playing lead guitar and sings in a small band. Music is how he met Julia who is a divine classical guitar player. Roger is the drummer of the band and lives in Mirabel. He is taking on his father's business that opened a locksmith shop forty years ago. Roger sees a large growth potential for the commercial and industrial side of his business. But locks and electronic security systems required for this market are far too complex for them to assume. Being already overloaded with residential customers, Roger has asked Gary to join him as a partner to lead their new commercial division. Gary analyzed the technology and knows he can master it. Knowing Roger's family and trusting them, he was nevertheless given the opportunity to look at their books and balance sheet. Seeing all is in order and promising, he accepted the challenge, considering his friendship as: 'an asset that he owns and that is worth more than the advancement he might get' with his present employer.

Try it!

Many new cars come equipped with a smart on-board computer that can link to the internet. The car dealer must check for updates to the software at each service call. Screens integrated into the dash, display essential driving messages and warnings. Even the display for the radio is smarter. It writes the name of the person being interviewed or the name of the song you listen to. For the past few weeks, I have noticed unexpected messages on the display. It did not happen often and, only when I was alone in the car so, I did not mention it to anybody, until now.

'Try it!' was the first strange message that came up. About to visit a potential customer, I had just parked in front of his building. My chances to make a sale to this person were slim. It took me a while to go in, debating if I should instead go visit my other regular customers in the area. The daring message encouraged me inside the building and this prospect surprised me. The manager agreed to see me without an appointment and invited me to follow him into his office. He was himself surprised to see me show-up at the same moment he decided to look for a supplier of my products. A few weeks later I had almost forgotten this 'Try it!' when a 'No' appeared on the same screen. While I was waiting at a red traffic light, I was thinking about staying where I have lived happily for ten years or moving one hundred kilometers away to live closer to friends that were moving out of town. Still thinking about this I noticed that the car screen had a big 'NO' flashing on it. So this 'NO' helped me decide to stay.

Many other useful messages came, giving me wise advice on different matters. Thinking back to identify when these messages started I could not find a date nor what caused them. Only last Saturday did I get a clue. I went to the cemetery to inspect and clean our family plot for the winter. My previous visit was last spring, on Mothers' Day, to plant daisies on my mother's grave. As I got back in my car the screen displayed 'Thank You and Come Again'. It is hard to believe but I comfort myself thinking that my numerous family members at the cemetery found this new way to help me. So I urge you to try it and let your departed loved ones give you counsel. All you have to do is park your car closer than one hundred meters from their grave so that this App can start to be active for you also. This way you can later secretly get their advice anywhere you are with your smart car.

Twister

Through the state of Utah, devastating twisters have shred away people's lives and belongings in a matter of minutes. Things got sucked-up and are known to have landed thousands of miles away. The Laredo family of six saved their lives in their underground shelter. It was next to their house, the house that used to be there in the small town of Bethel, Utah. The ordeal lasted no more than fifteen minutes and when it was quiet again outside, they cautiously came out of the shelter. They could not believe what they saw. The barn full of cattle, the house and their two cars were now in a pile of debris mixed with neighbors' farms scattered for miles.

Debbie and Jack Laredo luckily had good insurance coverage and were able to re-build on the same spot. This area had never been hit by such a storm and chances of being hit again were just as bad anywhere else. This all happened three years ago and they now decided to go on a vacation for a week. They had not taken time off together for ages and their family accepted to look after their kids while they were away. It took some discussion to select the destination but both agreed it would include horseback riding time because they both always enjoyed it.

Looking at a multitude of offers, they opted for a Dude Ranch, thirty miles west of Phoenix, in the Arizona desert. The 'Ok Coral' is an eight bedroom one storey ranch house operated as an Inn by two couples who live there. While it is a Ponderosa style building it offers comfortable and modern amenities. Debbie and Jack got settled-in and, with the help of Lorne the hired wrangler, selected their individual horse and saddle for the week. Soon they felt like kids again. After a healthy breakfast they would ride and admire the wonderful and spectacular scenery. After lunch in the shade of giant cacti, the afternoon was just as amazing as they returned to the ranch through different trails. On day four of their six-day holiday, while looking out from a view point, Debbie spotted something shining at the base of shrubs. Using a stick to scare away the snakes, Jack helped her free a three foot long plaque that looked familiar. Sure enough it was the plaque that had been over the top of the front door of their home and still read 'Laredo – In God We trust' and indeed they do.

WarmKle

Ankles and calves are sensitive to cold temperature and give you a lot of discomfort when not properly covered in winter. If you need to walk in a foot deep of snow, it gets even worse. Some men will wear long knee-high socks for that reason. I never could stand them because they are too warm to wear once you are inside, working in an office all day. Thighs are not as sensitive to cold and a layer of pants close to that skin is usually enough. But, with most pants falling straight down the leg, the fabric stands away, leaving the bare skin of the calf to freeze.

I love winter sports and when the sun shines on a cold -15°C with fresh snow, my favorite sport is cross-country skiing. Dressed warmly with light layers, you do not suffer from the cold and even build-up a good sweat as you climb hills. It is so wonderful to glide on a sparkling white snow trail while the sun angles its way through tall pine trees loaded with diamonds. All this with warm ankles and calves thanks to gaiters. This essential piece of equipment is weatherproof and snow will not adhere to them. So you can ski in deep snow or speed down a hill not worried that, should you go knee deep, you will still have warm ankles.

Coming back to work on a Monday morning after a beautiful Sunday of skiing, I felt the cold on my calves while I was de-icing the windshield of my car. So I thought of using the ski gaiters over my pants to keep my calves warm. They fit well and so snug over ski boots but they are difficult to use over work shoes and pants. The same night I thought of a solution and designed a pattern. The next night I stopped at a fabric store and bought a few yards of a charcoal grey weatherproof fabric along with some Velcro strips. Luckily my mother showed me how to use her sewing machine. She gave it to me when she passed away and I use it regularly. Stitching Velcro strips on specific spots of the fabric was easy. It's a cinch to wrap this protective layer around your ankles and calves before you walk out in the snow. They are as easy to remove once you are at the office and so small, they fit in your coat pockets. Women can also use them and store them in a purse. And that, ladies and gentlemen, is how the WarmKle came to be.

Nowhere

Out in the middle of nowhere lives the nowhere man. The Beatles made him famous by writing a song about him. Bert Zamboni is his name and he wisely stayed free from all this fame. Nowhere land is home for him, where he lives with Anny Nobody. He met her on a splendid sunny day while he was on one of his usual nowhere outings he likes so much. Anny was hitchhiking her way to another farm. He could not believe his luck. Anny had such a lovely body that he begged her to prove that Nobody was really her name. Sure enough, her ID showed that name. She is an expert apple picker. Following the apple picking season across America, she gets to work outside and feels free as a bird while doing what she likes the most.

On his way on a nowhere anyhow, he decided to join her picking. What a good team they became and soon they were in demand by most farmers. Apple growers favor working married couples by giving them better living quarters. Bert Zamboni did not care much about his surname so, he asked Anny to marry him and she was pleased by his request to change his name to Bert Nobody. It all happened in a non-denomination chapel on road 17 in Petawawa, Ontario. Determined to avoid highways, their honeymoon road trip lasted a long while. Apple growers from all over were anxious to meet the lucky man that the lovely Anny had chosen at last.

By the time they made it to Vancouver, we heard that Anny was pregnant. She had always been in top shape so she insisted to carry-on picking apples up to her fourth month. Bert at least got her to stop carrying heavy crates loaded with apples and let him move her ladder. Their lovely son was born safely and in honor of the newly elected prime minister of Canada, they named him Just. Growing fast the young boy is off to a great start with such caring parents and his ID proudly shows him as Just Nobody from Nowhere.

Hear The Beatles sing NowhereMan at:
https://www.youtube.com/watch?v=93rSXA8aeG4

Friendship

'La Place Publique' by Robert Élie was the name of the play in which they were both actors at high-school in 1971. The teachers had selected a good play because it required twenty-three actors. It was a challenge to keep the actors, chosen from amongst the school teenagers, serious about practices and interested enough to show up for the two or three presentations of the play. Through all these meetings is probably when Andrew and Max had met. They were not from the same neighborhood but had mutual friends.

Max was a year older so he went to college before Andrew. They would still meet regularly at friends' parties, playing hockey, baseball or on camping trips. They were both from good functional families but could not afford to pay for university. Max worked hard at week-end and night jobs and, even joined the army for one year to finally complete a PhD in Psychology. Andrew did not have that talent but started working in sales and liked it so much that he made a successful career of it. Each had various girlfriends but Max married Gloria, whom he had met at high-school, while Andrew married Sophie, his boss's secretary. The two couples became even better friends later and helped each other set-up their first apartment and houses. The four of them were anxious to see the world so they made a plan to tour Europe for one year. When they were all about twenty six years old, each couple had a new motorhome paid in full, and had them crane lifted and secured on the back deck of the Alexander Pushkin cruise ship. They set sail from Montreal and, landed in Germany ten days later. They toured Western Europe for nine months and came back to resume their lives. Their individual work careers went well enough that at age 57 they were all retired. So here they are, Andrew and Max, in a superb Florida resort riding their bikes at 8:30am while chatting and laughing. This is how they start most mornings, on their way to play tennis outside during five winter months and making the most of 44 years of friendship. No one has too many of such trustworthy friends. They find it sometimes difficult to perpetuate this but they are all very proud when their precious friendship has survived another year.

Felix

Nathalie loves cats and now lives with two of them. Her former husband was allergic so they lived together twelve years without pets. Nathalie always had cats as a child, so when she divorced, she had up to four of them for a while. She plays bridge every week and was asked by a few friends to take care of their pets and their house while they were away on vacation. At age fifty-five she lost her job when the company closed and she had a hard time finding new permanent work. Still in need of income before retirement, she got proper insurance coverage and started a formal house caring business.

Within two years, she had over fifty regular customers and had to hire an assistant to avoid losing new ones. She also realised that she had not taken any time off for her own vacation. Her relatives in Europe were used to seeing her every two or three years. Once Linda her assistant was properly trained, Nathalie left on vacation for the whole month of September in Europe. That is the quietest month for her business so she was sure that Linda would not be overworked. In order to get cheaper plane tickets, she booked her trip months in advance.

Hans, her uncle lives in a large villa close to Salzburg, Austria. He and his wife Greta were going on a cruise to Asia for the month of September. When they heard that Nathalie was coming, they offered her the opportunity to live in their house. She gladly accepted and would also take care of their dog and cat. Hans and Greta told their friends and neighbors about Nathalie so they would not worry if they saw her around their house. Sure enough, if some of them also wanted to go away, they got her to care for their house and pets. Seeing that this service was highly in demand, she hired a manager based in Salzburg to run her European operations. Nathalie now heads a two hundred employee company with offices in Montreal, Salzburg, Paris, New York and Chicago. Felix is the name of her house care company in memory of her first cat.

Emergence

It never occurred to him that it was so. He always liked to walk for hours on a long sandy beach. The Atlantic Ocean beaches were the ones he visited the most, being the closest to his home town, Montreal, Quebec. Over the years he had walked ocean front beaches in Maine, Massachusetts, Virginia and Florida. Not much of a swimmer, he would mostly walk the beach and sit on a chaise-longue to read a good novel while listening to the tempo of the waves.

His beach accommodations have varied greatly over time. A campground was all that he could afford the first time. Located away from prime land, you needed a car to get to the beach. Then you wasted a lot of time to find a parking space giving access to an over-crowded section of the beach, being the closest to the parking lot. Years later, he made it to Virginia Beach. In order to be more comfortable, he rented a tent-trailer and hauled it all the way there, hitched to his new Gremlin. The campground there was next to the beach and he really enjoyed the easy access to it. His girlfriend on that trip became his wife soon afterwards. Combining their income, they sought more comfort on their next vacation. The condo apartment they rented was directly on the beach. Both the living-room and their bedroom had large windows facing the Atlantic.

The first morning, at about 6am, a strange sight woke him up in a panic. He sleeps better in a dense darkness so the drapes were pulled tight. But now, such a strong red glow was seeping from the top and the sides of the curtains, it looked like the outside was on fire. He got up quickly to check what was going on. The sun was at full strength rising out of the ocean and was backed by a bright blue sky. Not every morning had a clear enough sky to allow this wonderful show but they loved watching the preamble and the gradual apparition of the sun. Over the years they thought they had seen it all but just yesterday, friends invited them for dinner in their ocean front condo. After dinner while they were having a nightcap on the balcony, the moon surprised them just as much when it emerged from the black and wavy horizon.

Humanity

Any oppressing power over people should beware that in so-doing, the oppressed will become stronger and eventually be able to surpass the oppressor. African-Americans, descendants of slaves can be a good example of this. Only the toughest and smartest slaves could survive their cruel existence. Survival genes are still present in their descendants giving them the potential to outperform others.

Not being black myself, I can only relate to what I have learned or experienced. Co-workers or friends who endured difficult periods in their life, always seem to have an edge. Sports team players and the military, if not hurt seriously, will remain cool-headed when facing stress or know when to duck to avoid a hit. Childhood probably has the most important impact. A loving and caring household is so important. Knowing it is a safe haven where you are always welcome is such a necessity but unfortunately, only a privilege.

Too bad that a lot of our being is based on luck! Anyone who is bragging about his superiority should realize that if you are born in a war zone or in an overpopulated refugee camp, your way to well-being is longer and hardly accessible. With the internet showing the well-off to even remote areas of the planet, families can see how others live and decide to migrate. Media are helping to inform us more about other races and cultures. This, added to an increasing level of education, gives our generation and subsequent ones, a chance to better appreciate and not be afraid of different races. Using my limited exposure to the world as an example, I notice that people of varied ethnicity can relate well. What seriously worries neighbours is when newcomers dress or shape their house too differently and barricade them in unsettling ways. But the most intolerable is when religious beliefs are used to treat women as a lower caste of human beings, not allowed equal rights. Women of today possess stronger survival genes and must be helped to pursue their crusade to save us before the other half self-destructs humanity.

Sneakers

John Pringle walks to school every morning. He almost wore his new green sneakers but changed at the last minute. He is only ten years old but already conscious about his looks. Along with his blue jacket and beige pants, he figured that his beige sneakers were a better fit. Feeling well after a big bowl of cereals and a load of fresh blueberries for breakfast, he is looking forward to his day in school. He is not that enthusiastic about it usually but today, Barak Obama himself will give a speech in front of all students. Recent statistics have shown that his school is the one from where originates the largest number of family doctors. In the constant challenge to solve the lack of family doctors all over the country, President Obama came to promote this school's efforts.

John's mother was proud to see her son being able to meet the President of the United States in person. John will never forget when by chance he was in the row where the President walked to exit and came to shake his hand. She prepared John's preferred dinner to celebrate the event. It was cream of mushroom as an appetizer and a huge juicy roast beef for the main course. His father and two sisters were all ears to let John describe the conference. Some of it was televised and sure enough, his magic moment with the President was shown. His mother had luckily recorded it so they were all able to watch it again all together in the evening.

Even the family rooster sensed that it was a special day. His vocalizing informed all the neighboring farms of how excited they all were. John was tired from this long day but made sure he brushed and whitened his teeth before going to bed. Tomorrow he will again be popular as one of the lucky few to have made such a close encounter with the President. His mind is made up to study hard and become a family doctor, counting on the support and expertize of his outstanding school. And to meet his classmates, he will wear his new polo shirt and slacks to fit the glee of his new cool green sneakers.

Dreamland

It all happened so fast, he was probably dreaming. While casually walking he went from Canada, to England, to France, to Morocco and even China. In each country he walked through some of their individual most beautiful sites. In France, he had lunch in a lovely Bistro called Patisserie des Halles. He even recalls when a little later, his wife Helen, bought a beautifully embroidered shirt in China. She intends to wear it for her Tai-Chi sessions. Later that day, they stopped in what looked like a movie theatre. But this dream remained wild and the three hundred or so seats started moving through a jungle loaded with dinosaurs. Before they got hurt, they managed to escape and went soaring over California.

This must have exhausted him because it was followed by a blank period where he probably slept deeply. Not long afterwards, his dream sat him in a Jeep with ten other strangers for a safari in Africa. Everybody remained quiet to avoid awakening the lions pretending to sleep in the jungle only thirty feet away from them. Like in any dream, your imagination is limitless. His own made huge parrots, owls, eagles and vultures come fly only inches over his head so he could admire them better. Then almost a hundred birds of various sizes got together singing and dancing in a twenty-minute musical show. After a while in Kidami Village, he noticed that animals were used to having dreamers around them. He was able to eat dinner with his wife at an exquisite table on ground level, close to a window with a great view. A few feet away, giraffes, ostriches and zebras were grazing peacefully.

He woke up totally lost in a strange room. He managed to find his way to the bathroom and back to bed. His mind was still primed and he found himself in the south of France. While sitting at the terrace of a cafe, he found himself in the middle of an action movie with a car chase and bandits firing at each other. Running away from the scare he hid in a car. Once the gun shots stopped, he looked around and noticed that all the cars parked in this area were full of people eating while watching a movie in a drive-in theatre. This slower period did not last long because he ran into Indiana Jones who was fighting German soldiers. Helen pulled him away from trouble to the Grand Floridian Hotel where they were greeted by a Christmas Choir. They elected to stay there and ate a lovely dinner followed by magnificent fireworks in Magic Kingdom, just across the lake.

MoonShine

A newly discovered lightness of being is optimized by better awareness of the obvious. This is quite an accomplishment when you live with the same spouse for over thirty years and both feel the same about it. A lot of 'been there, done that' can surface easily. Like most couples with a bucket list, they strive to get it all done while they still can. That is how Judy and Dave try to live happily, the ever after part of it.

Now that their three kids are raising their own children and are very busy with their careers, Judy and Dave see them all only four times a year. These gatherings always last one week. To be all together, they share the rental cost of a big house. Not everybody can stay the whole week but they all manage to be there together for a few days. The balance of the year is quieter but they have a lot of friends to play cards, tennis, go cycling or bowling.

Two years ago, Judy and Dave joined a few friends in a resort in Florida. During their two weeks stay, they liked it so much, they decided to buy a small property. They now avoid cold winters and spend five months a year in this tropical paradise, surrounded by a new group of friends. Florida offers many attractions and they now have visited most of them. Of course they have visited Disney a dozen times or so with their children and now with grandchildren. Judy loves fireworks and she is always ready to go back to Disney to see more of them.

This year Dave rented a huge house in Cocoa Beach facing the Atlantic. They would spend most mornings wide awake to watch the magic of the sun rising out of the ocean. Today, they all went for dinner at a Thai restaurant, a few blocks away. They went early at 4:30pm to make sure they would not be late for the evening show. At 5:50pm they walked to the end of the Cocoa Beach Jetty, stretching about a quarter mile in the ocean. The show started with the sunset, painting the sky with psychedelic colours. Dolphins then danced out of the water to glimpse at it, while pelicans came flying below radar, following their squadron leader back to base for the night. Then stars started turning-on as dusk was dimming-off the sun. With their Thai dinner, Judy and Dave drank some good Sake but, it felt like they had drunk something wild when the full moon suddenly rose straight out of the pitch dark Atlantic ocean and delivered an impressive doze of MoonShine.

Monday

For so many years at school and later at work, Monday meant going back to serious responsibilities after a week-end of fun. George was slowly getting rid of this feeling and he is now giving a fully optimistic view on an upcoming Monday. When he retired a few years ago, he started to play tennis more often. He will never be the best player but he plays well enough to be in a league with the good players. His other leisure activities are cycling, walking and reading.

George had to travel out of town for his work on most weeks. Because of this he could never be present enough to join a league for most activities in his home town. While on the road, visiting customers in other cities, he occupied some of his free evenings by attending a baseball or soccer game being played close to his hotel or, he would go bowling. In the past, smoking was allowed while bowling. George could not stand the smell and rarely bowled. Still he liked it a lot and now that he is no longer a nomad, he decided to have a look at River Lane Bowling.

The universe that he discovered there really dazzled him. A restaurant and bar on site allowed you to eat very well while watching forty bowling lanes. Just after lunch a lot of players started to practise and by one o'clock, most lanes were busy with teams of four players. George liked what he saw so much that he asked to join the league. One team player had back surgery and George was invited to replace him. George showed up the next week, early enough to bowl two games of practice and met Paul, Duane and Steve, his teammates. The beauty of it all is that George is now part of about one hundred pleasant retired folks, all out to have a good time and make the most of a Monday afternoon. He now enjoys this weekly activity so much that he surprises himself thinking, 'Thank God it's Monday'.

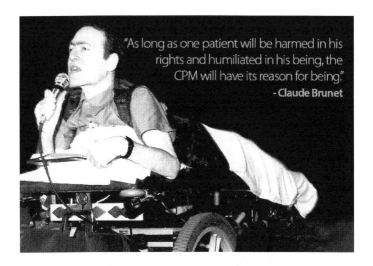

"As long as one patient will be harmed in his rights and humiliated in his being, the CPM will have its reason for being."
- Claude Brunet

Dignity

Disgusted to witness it repeatedly, he decided that it was enough and that he had to intervene. A minimum of dignity for people like him, with severe disabilities, should not be an excessive expectation in a rich country like Canada. With some friends, living hospitalized all the time because they required more care than what is possible at home, they formed a committee in 1974. Fully aware of population upheavals in the 1960's seeking greater freedom and more justice, it inspired their mission. Their 'Marathon du Sourire' on a wide boulevard of downtown Montreal, gathered dozens of disabled but determined people. Helped by volunteers and media presence, they signified to the world that they too exist.

Armed with his smile and well thought-out messages, Claude has earned the respect of the people, governments and unions that worked for the well-being of patients. In the 1970's devoted religious having been replaced by unionized employees, some workers with muscled arms and loud mouths have placed their acquired right to strike before essential patient care. In court, Claude and members of his CPM (Council for the protection of patients) won several class suits, requesting a minimum of respect from too many that lacked it almost completely.

Claude Brunet, my big brother died in 1988 but his work was so important that many volunteers have kept it alive for now over 40 years. Through the CPM website www.cpm.qc.ca all permanently hospitalized patients in Quebec are in constant contact with a competent team, led by my youngest brother Paul to help them. Several other parts of the world are inspired by the CPM because everywhere, dignity of the human is at risk. May we always remain sensitive to the needs of the most helpless so that they can retain their ultimate resource that is, to nevertheless still smile.

Destiny

Destiny struck again in St-Pete. Olga and her husband Karsten live in Munich, Germany. Olga's godmother had left Germany twenty years ago to retire with friends in a beautiful resort in Virginia Beach. All of them being avid golfers, they also owned condos in another golf resort in St-Petersburg, Florida. This way they could play almost every day of the year, even in winter.

Olga had always kept phone contact at least once a month with her godmother. Still she was surprised when a notary called informing her that godmother had died and she was her only heir. Olga was deeply saddened by losing her. She had been like a mother to her. Olga was only eleven when her mother died. Now with her husband Karsten, they had just got back home a week ago, returning from a cruise in Asia. They have built a jewellery business over the past fifteen years. The cruise was to celebrate the sale of their business, the proceeds of which will be paid to them over the next five years.

They flew in from Munich on a direct flight to Washington, DC and drove to her Godmother's house in Virginia Beach. Olga was familiar with this lovely house, having stayed there on vacation many times. But they found it too big to maintain and after a few days of living in it, they selected a real estate agent to put it up for sale and, left for St-Pete. Not knowing in what shape the condo in St-Pete would be, they found a bed & breakfast in the historic district of the town.

At 8:30am next morning, they showed up for breakfast and sat at a nicely set table for two by the window.

This is where we met them, a few minutes later. My wife and I said good-morning and introduced ourselves before sitting at the table next to theirs. The four of us were the only guests, so we started chatting. They were amazed to meet us and hear about our good life in Quebec, just as much as we were to hear about their life in the Black Forest of Germany. We discussed a few world matters and destinations enough to notice that we shared similar views. Even if the condo in St-Pete is reputed to be in a very elegant setting, they expect to sell it as well and use the money to select an area more to their liking. They envied our retired life barefoot in sandals most of the year. Who knows, destiny may get our paths to cross again one day.

Lifetime

Most of what we buy must be replaced eventually. Wear and tear or fashion is the probable terminator. But what about the Lifetime Map Update option that I purchased with my GPS? Sure enough the fine print states the limit is the life of the GPS or the life of the original owner, whichever comes first.

Now that we have celebrated the tenth anniversary of our lifetime companionship, we are at risk of technological change. Just like my still operational eight track tape player, my GPS will surely get replaced by some kind of iPod or similar, smarter and incompatible device. Making the most of it while it works, as usual before leaving for a long drive, I connected my GPS to my computer to process a map update. This procedure is amazing. Imagine all the printed maps that I would need to carry to show all roads of North America. It usually takes one hour to download the update. But this time, it took three hours. I suspected a connection loss or heavier than usual traffic on the server of the GPS manufacturer. Luckily at the end, I got a green screen with the long awaited 'Successful Download' confirmation message.

Making sure that the GPS was working correctly, I turned it on to test it while on my way to the grocery store. It properly displayed the streets and gave vocal instructions for upcoming turns. But my wife and I were really surprised when the GPS asked us to give it our shopping list. I told her it must be a new feature that came with the update. She decided to play along and recited all the items. When she mentioned milk, the GPS asked what kind and she replied a two litre with 1% fat. The GPS instantly replied: Walmart is currently out but IGA and Provigo have it and, gave similar comments on other items. We could hardly believe it but later that day, I read that this new feature allows to check most major stores stock in real time. But the most amazing new feature is, believe it or not, the detection of a highway overpass, upcoming collapse location so that you can drive away from it and, optimize 'Your' Lifetime option.

Addison

Once upon the bridge, Henry nearly fell into the canal. One of the rotten wood planks broke, and his foot crashed right through it. Luckily his wife Audrey was holding his hand and helped him back up. Both of them are 88 years old and still in good enough shape to join some of our Nature Trail Walks. The Addison Trail snakes its way under palm and oak trees that have been growing on a berm. It was formed while digging the Addison Canal more than one hundred years ago.

Betty is guiding our group of fifteen happy retirees, out for a friendly walk while enjoying this magnificent morning in the Central Florida wilderness. We all cautiously crossed the bridge and made sure Henry was fine. He said he was part of the team who repaired this bridge ten years ago. He no longer felt strong enough to fix it again.

Don, Jim and I offered to join forces and do the work. One hundred planks of wood had to be pre-cut and carried to site over a distance of one mile. Jim offered his Jeep but did not find a dirt road to reach the canal. It took a few weeks but Sandy obtained a permit allowing us to open a gate and drive the Jeep on a dirt road located on a fenced state conservation area.

A day before the job, Jim and I went to buy the wood and had it cut to length. Back at my house, we pre-drilled four holes in each of the one hundred planks before loading them back in his Jeep. The next morning, Don joined us and it was a rough ride but Jim's Jeep took us to the bridge. While Don and Jim removed the rotten planks, I repaired a section of one of the two wood street pole used as the bridge structure for over 20 years. The three of us rarely use tools in this lovely resort where we snowbird the winter. So we had to borrow hammers, pry-bars and nail pouches from neighbours. Some of them now live all year in Florida and have impressive handymen tool sheds.

Sandy manages the Nature Center. At 11am she walked the trail alone while texting on her smartphone, and arrived in time to see us install the last planks and load the rotten wood in the Jeep. She took a picture of our bridge repair team. We stood as a happy crew at midway across the bridge, proud to have given the bridge another ten years of safe crossing.

PomPom

Out of nowhere, he just shows-up. His camouflage is so perfect that all you see is movement. Then, in order to give you a good look, he will stop and stare. Now that he is close enough, his senses are all primed to evaluate you and the danger of his surroundings. They say his eyesight is not the greatest but his large ears never miss a beat. And his nose is so active and appraisingly twitching that he probably knows if you are currently sweating or not.

Neighbourly and friendly, he gladly shares your backyard with blue jays, cardinals, robins and squirrels. Everyone is minding his own business but it is obvious that love is in the air. Trees go out of their way to launch the spring. Fully frilled with buds, they emit a subtle green glow. Naked brown and black branches proudly show their own buds to avoid being trimmed as dead wood. Shady areas are bordered by a white lacework of snow. The sun exposed lawn by the fence has gathered hundreds of dead leaves, piled up as a comfortable mat with as many shades of brown.

This is where our friend likes to hangout. He blends so well with the leaves that he safely stays there for hours. Smartly, this is where he positioned the main entrance to his home. A large log keeps the top steady and straight. He simply dug under and made his way while eating tasty little roots of the giant maple tree. Noticing how well he relates with birds, we have installed three bird houses around his loft. They seem to rely on each other to sound the alarm if a predator shows-up. Air traffic is now heavier almost as much as on the ground. Robins aerate the grass by picking for worms. Squirrels with loaded jowls proudly parade with a nut or two. Meanwhile our cottontail friend bids us farewell by showing-off his white bouncy PomPom.

Watch

Clockwise or Counterclockwise, that is the question. A clever young man using his smart phone would probably look for an App to check it. Digital displays, the widely spread norm for today's clocks will be useless to know which way to twist the cap. But his favorite jar of blueberry jam is stuck. He remembers at school learning to turn counterclockwise to open or loosen things. He then could look at the classroom wall clock or the clock in his mother's kitchen for reference.

Now as a young adult sharing a four bedroom apartment with three other students, none of them have a clock with a rotating hand. Living close to the university campus is so convenient and lively. But this is where he would never wear an analog watch on his wrist anyway because it is considered so passé. Suddenly, he remembered that there is a clock on the church steeple across the street. Looking out of his living room window, he noticed that it must be defective, for its hands were not moving and showing two-thirty when it was now eight-fifteen on his phone. Already late for school, he left without having any jam on his toast.

As he attended five classes today, it remained at the back of his mind. He would hate having to break the jar to get to the jam. But he would hate even more admitting to his friends that he has this problem. Going through his day on campus, he noticed that all wall clocks had gone digital. Could it be so that most students could graduate and not be sure which way the clock hands used to turn? Considering it not an essential matter, he stopped thinking about it. At the end of his classes he got lucky while riding the elevator in the science building. An old man close to him had his arms crossed over his chest. John noticed his watch and the clockwise movement of the needle hand. As soon as he got home, he ran the jam jar under hot water and managed to turn the cover counterclockwise. But what if he forgets again? What else other than his phone can help him? Sitting on the toilet thinking about it, he later had a good laugh noticing the water turning clockwise and simultaneously flushed away his problem.

Peace

Religions are all based on the love of God and respect of all living creatures. But mankind has put aside kindness whilst using religions to dominate and conquer territories. Hate and revenge have infected genes of many afflicted generations and are rooted in the mindset of too many extremists. People of various faiths have, luckily for us, decided to stop going into religious wars. Islam has also evolved but so many fundamentalists remain in the middle-age era. Dress codes and strict rules for social interactions still have women stoned for disobeying.

What happened to Peace & Love that changed most of the world in the 1970s? Fuelled by Flower Power, it got a few generations to banish differences and glorify kindness. The internet and the media were not as omnipresent as today. Countries were blocking the information. But The Beatles still infiltrated and had some level of influence on everyone with their song Give Peace A Chance. Now that borders are easier to cross in Europe, even Russia is more open for business but, many challenges remain. The poorest people of the world can now see on TV how others live on the planet. The flow of migrants is so great that the Trumps of this world want to put up new walls, emphasizing their dominance and self-interest.

Just like terrorists use the internet to recruit, why can't Islam issue positive propaganda for peace? Pope Francis is doing a great job at it. Hopefully Islamic leaders of rich Arab countries will give help to migrants like he did. It was very impressive to see the Vatican provide asylum to twelve Islamic migrants. We are all influenced by our surroundings. We watch the news and get a short daily dose of the world crisis. Most movies are loaded with guns and crimes. The time has come to Give Peace another chance. Writers must all flood the media with kindness for the ultimate sake of mankind.

Tarp

Every new day can be wonderful. We must all make the most of this privilege to live a new one while we can. That is the way I see it to honor my numerous family departed loved ones who did not get to live as old as I. An agenda helps us remember appointments and commitments. When none of these dictate our actions, the To-Do list takes over. Of course sometimes, the weather will force postponement of activities outdoors. Now, with all this considered, only one day of the year scores as my favorite. Family gatherings for Christmas, New Year's Eve and birthdays score very high. The same goes for outings with friends on a camping trip. We have not been cycling much lately but we also enjoy riding for a day with friends out on small country roads. This scores even with a day out sailing on Lake St-Louis. Of course, our days of walking on the beach and playing in the waves at Cocoa Beach Florida are memorable. At the other extreme, cross-country skiing on immaculate new snow loaded with diamonds like flakes under a bright blue sky is fantastic. It is also very pleasant to play tennis for hours in a foursome of friends that change regularly. Still, only one day gets my vote as favourite year after year.

It falls rarely on the same date because of the weather. Most years, late April will be nice enough for it to happen. The forecast day temperature for the next few days must be above 10°C and nights above freezing. It cannot be delayed too much to avoid crawling bugs nesting. Usually we will start that day at 10am, when the sun is out and strong enough to avoid heavy clothes. This year it was on April 30 and the trees were still leafless but decorated with millions of buds. While the area is clear of foliage we can see better so, we plant new shrubs and trees to embellish our landscape. Optimizing the mid afternoon sun, we use the patio space, still free of the stored chairs and patio table and, we brush it clear of debris. Then I remove bricks that hold the bottom of the tarps in place against the winter wind. Loosening wall clamps I can now remove the tarps that cover our screened summer solarium. This very simple action represents our reconnection with nature's bud-bursting eruption giving us a new reborn type of boost, enough to score as our favorite day of the year.

Flour

This Sunday morning was so busy at the local florist. Flower arrangements at various prices were ready for pick-up. Knowing that my mother did not have a flower vase in her hospital room, I selected one from the florist. The flower girl offered a perfectly sized flower pot. The flower stems were just long enough to stand and form a beautiful bouquet.

My wife Gloria was at home cooking meanwhile. Whole grain flour only was used, following the recipe to bake my mother's favorite cookies. We will all visit her at tea time on this Mother's Day afternoon. It took a while for the doctor to detect what had intoxicated her. His first guess was that she had inhaled too much flour that flew off the board when a sudden draft blew from the window over the kitchen sink. She did not explain before she fainted. On the phone with the lady who answered her call to 911, all she had time to mention was what sounded like flower but, did she mean flour? The superintendent of her apartment building had to open her door for the emergency crew to get to her. They noticed the flour on the kitchen counter, next to the baking pan. Her neighbor and friend Martha came over when she heard all the commotion in the hallway. She explained that they both spent the last few days caring for their flowers in the community garden across the street.

The ambulance rushed her to the hospital and informed the medical team that their patient may be allergic to pollen that was omnipresent currently in this area. They also had to mention that as she fell, she probably knocked off her flour sack. It was spread over a large area. Let's hope that it will not have damaged the fine flower motif embroidery in the carpet under the dining room table.

The four of us travelled together to visit her in the hospital. The head nurse rushed to stop us from entering her room. The doctor was still not sure if she was sick because of flower or flour so he asked that we do not let her close to flowers like the ones we brought to her. Still she was happy to see us all and really appreciated having some of her favorite cookies that Gloria had made for her. I had brought a thermos of hot water so I made her favorite infusion of hibiscus flower tea. She was about halfway through her first cup when her eyes rolled over and we had to ring for help.

It is only a few days later that our mother was able to recall what had really happened. Following instructions of Doctor Chi in his TV show, she used her flower sifter to produce flower flour with rose petals she had dried in her toaster-oven. But suddenly the sifter jammed and she got a nose full load of flower flour up her face. Some of it also got into her eyes and she could barely see when she dialed 911 before passing out. The Police kept her under surveillance for a few more days while they checked her computer and her activities for the past few weeks. Now assured that she was not dealing drugs, they still warned her that they would keep an eye on her dangerous business. The doctor is the one that involved the drugs squad because he said that if this rose petal flower flour had been Never Bleach Flour, it would have been lethal.

Thank God the Police did not know that the 'Groovy with PFFP' logo on her T-Shirt meant Pot Flower Flour Power.

Weather

As years go by we forget how some things can gain importance often out of our control. Theo had no clue about this when he initiated this process. He had been working as a stationary engineer for an apple grower's cooperative. His main duty was to make sure the enormous industrial boiler would always be ready to supply steam for the apple juice bottling plant. For over forty years he helped them grow the business by his machines maintenance expertise.

Father of five daughters and four sons, he worked very hard at keeping this job at the plant, so conveniently located just across from his house on main street. Once all children were of school age, his wife Olivine started working part time on the assembly line to bring-in much needed extra income to feed this hungry platoon of kids. Twelve hours a day would be his average but he would even have to sleep on site during the fall crops overload.

Soon enough, Theo was honored by the coop as another twenty five years of service employee. As a memoralia, the company offered a stylish barometer with a little plaque. Theo was so proud; he placed it well in view in his living room. Over years, the children all moved away and the parents moved to smaller accommodations. We were always amazed to see this globe format barometer get the prime spot wherever they lived. My wife and I were so honored to hang it next to the fireplace in our living room, now that we have inherited it. The quality instrument dates back to 1970 but still gives reliable information about temperature, humidity and atmospheric pressure. Its unique globe format is interesting to look at even if smart phones are easier to use.

Will Way

As the saying goes, when there is a will, there is a way. It all started in 1663 when the Sulpician François d'Urfé founded a parish on what is now known as the Town of Baie-D'Urfé. Mostly farmland for a long while, George Edward Fritz operated his farm that extended from the lake front. The Town of Baie-D'Urfé acquired it from his succession in 1979. The last will drafted by Fritz has suggested that the Town should dedicate the farmland only for community needs. It could not be sold to a promoter to build mansions or be piled up with condos. Baie-D'Urfé being a small municipality of 3,900 residents, privately owned businesses could not build and make a profit from operating social amenities. The area is so lovely that citizens gladly volunteer to staff most functions required at town events. Over the years, residents have always voted favourably when the Town council suggested building cultural and sports facilities. Using small portions of the vast Fritz farmland, now stand a library, a pool, a community centre, a curling club, tennis courts and a sailing marina, all managed by volunteer members of these not-for-profit club entities. Members' children also join the Clubs' junior teams. Members who are lucky enough to retire still in good health come to play almost every day.

Aging locally is the ultimate goal of these volunteers. Their houses are now too big for their retirement needs but, they remain in them because they like the area so much. Alternatives that they have considered and visited are mainly condos in areas too crowded, too noisy and more expensive than living in their old houses. So they remain in them as long as they can. After a few more years, running short of funds, they postpone repairing the roof, the driveway, the windows and the landscape. So many of such houses now fall into a state of disrepair that the Town has to offer a solution.

Imagine that the Town wisely used the Will Way to help its long-time supportive volunteers. Selecting a discrete area of the wide open space left by Fritz, they made sure that no existing house would be drastically affected. The Town owned two-storey apartment building's low height would not shade any other property, nor would it block a view. So the population attended two information sessions and councillors voted to change the zoning of a section of this farmland that had become a park, to allow the construction of a twenty-four unit apartment building. Named Club-D'Urfé, this location allows residents to live only a short walking distance from the amenities they so cherish and sustained for so long. Retirees can now rent a 1,600 sq.ft. three-bedroom apartment and sell their house. In most cases, the sale price frees enough capital that once invested, generates income covering most of the rental cost. Their capital is now theirs to enjoy the Good Life while not worrying about a house. In a decade or two or when their health requires more assisted living, they will gladly move to the Maxwell Residence and still live locally. In the meantime, Club-D'Urfé offers a pleasant retirement, even in winter, thanks to its 40 x 240 feet atrium embellished by lovely plants and loads of daylight. Future generations rest assured because Club-D'Urfé is an ideal solution for aging in wonderful Baie-D'Urfé, Quebec.

Mindset

It is so strange how it affects me that I have to write about it. I cannot help but wonder if most of my life was under the same influence. Why is it that I now officially detect, at age 63 this trigger-like key to my mindset? If it is a side effect of being in my fifth year of retirement, then so be it.

Aging healthily is such a privilege. Not necessarily dependent on wealth makes it another rare element of fairness in our sometimes ruthless world. Cats with their nine lives can waste a few but I feel I must make the most of mine, probably the only one in this used shell. So, now that time is on my side for a while, I try to optimize it. Lucky enough to live in a safe and beautiful part of the world, I do not feel the urge to fill a bucket list or run around the globe. My family and friends live close enough that we can be together in a day. Paying attention to the world in my close vicinity is extremely fulfilling. Meeting and chatting with people in person beats any computer virtual enhancement. Running into each other while out for a walk or in the park spurs many elements of surprise. Setting a time and date to be together for a few hours is what I prefer. Having put aside other concerns, our minds get in-sync and can attain another level of beatitude, only given to team players.

For long periods of our life, we do not really have a say in selecting the people who surround us. Our parents and other kin mold our base in a variety of good and bad ways. Students and teachers are also imposed upon us in our school years. This schooling period is important because it represents our first chance to befriend our own selection of people. If you are lucky, some of them will remain your friends for life and influence your personality.

But language is the switchgear I have now uncovered. Without consciously driving it, I realize that I am a fairly different person when I speak French or English. All my life I have spoken French and carry with it all this beingness. My youth, while speaking French only, was saddened by a lot of death and sickness in the family. I was exposed to English most of my life but only started speaking it regularly in my twenties. My adulthood was happier and less tragedy happened while speaking English. Now fairly fluent in both languages, I think in each and do not translate while I speak or write. It must be a wild experience to be as fluent in three or four. Would it be like having many heads to select from every morning?

Rio

None of this should have happened, but it did. George had a strange feeling all morning and reminded himself he should have been more cautious. His wife Lisa had warned him weeks before. George had discussed the matter with her to pick her brain and seek her seasoned womanly intuition. Her verdict was clear. George had to make it to the Rio 2016 Olympics.

Lisa and George had travelled to Europe and Asia but never to South America. Most of their trips piggybacked along with George's work. As a journalist for the CBC, he was sent all over to report on political events. When he was posted in cities that Lisa wanted to visit, she would fly in and join him for a few days. They both were avid cyclists and as soon as the 'must see sites' in town were visited, they would ride to the countryside. Using their broad network of contacts, they would stay with friends of a friend with an extra room. They got to meet locals this way, not just tourists, and blend firsthand in people's daily living.

George was now 55 years old and looking for a new challenge. CBC, his employer, had a good opinion of his work and valued greatly his knowledge of how politics work. He was honoured when CBC offered George the position of Morning Man for their popular radio show. His fame opened doors and he had an easier access for interviewing key people in the news. For the Rio Olympics, CBC had to select ten journalists on their staff to cover the events. Most of them wanted to go and seniority was playing against George. Both he and Lisa wanted so much to go that he leveraged his key contacts and made the CBC team. Playing it safe, they flew in separate groups of two.

But George and Lisa never left Montreal. He had to wait in line at the passport office for a last-minute renewal. Someone must have had a bad case of diarrhea. George started to be sick the same night and Lisa followed the next morning. CBC had to replace George who was out of shape for a week and contagious for one more. The good side of this is that George and Lisa got to watch all of the games on TV while they were forced to stay home to get better. Visiting Rio will be for later but they will always remember it as their best Olympics since it was their first ever total viewing of all events.

Ottawa

Once Kevin got there, he thought: 'may as well make the most of it'. Ottawa was not his first choice but it was only a two-hour drive from his family and friends in Montreal. With his new degree in computer engineering he first found a job in Pointe-Claire. A few years later, he could not resist the offer he received from a major corporation in Ottawa. This was also his first move out of his parents' home into his own apartment.

Passionate about his work in the fast-evolving telecom world, many days, the only time he made it to his flat was to sleep. Talented and dedicated as he was to put in long hours, he quickly became a team leader. Too busy to get seriously involved he, like most others, had lots of girlfriends. The majority of his acquaintances were also from out of town. Probably half of Ottawa residents had migrated recently to Canada. The federal government encourages this influx of new talent by enforcing a 'minimum ratio of immigrants' hiring policy. Private companies have also followed this trend and take advantage of their eagerness to perform in Canada.

Reluctant to mingle with foreigners at first, his perspective evolved and he soon appreciated the kaleidoscope of personalities around him. The ones he met most frequently came from India, China, Bangladesh, Holland and Portugal. When he reached 35, he decided to get married, buy a house and start a family. Within a year he found a good-looking bride with a similar plan. They had mutual friends and knew each other very well. The three-bedroom cottage they bought together required major renovations. So busy at this on top of their day job, they postponed having children. It was a good thing because their marriage turned sour. For six years he had to fight and pay dearly his way out of it.

Colleagues at work saved him. They introduced him to a lovely woman from India. Her family had been in Ottawa for more than thirty years. Everybody confirmed that they were a great match so they figured that a few years of courting was enough. She was 36 and he was 43 on their wedding day. Celebrations started at her parents' house with 80 of their closest relatives for dinner and dancing in a park next door. Both have a very successful career so they decided to go all out and invite 175 guests to their prestigious traditional Indian wedding two days later. Relatives and friends flew in from all over the world to salute their union. She was his only daughter and she had never been married so, her father was very proud to see her so happy. Guests had dressed-up for the event. It was a beautiful gathering of people in awe of such refinement, and even the weather looked its best to bless their union in Ottawa.

Original ?

When you feel that all is said and done, that is when it can begin. Writing everyday builds the skill and maintains an interesting level of fluidity in the stream of ideas. But each morning the fear of redundancy sneaks-in a little more. It is so impressive to think that our brain can sort it all out and keep us from repeating ourselves. There has to be a limit but I cannot believe that I have already covered every square millimetre of my storytelling ability.

Commenting on a new event is a sure way to avoid repetition. But history has a tendency of repeating itself. People and location can be different but sure enough, each generation can make the same mistakes. If only this aspect had been emphasized, all of us would have been more attentive to history class at school. YouTube and Wikipedia in a sense have become the reference base for our present era. For just about any topic, you can read about it or watch a video that can influence your decision for a pending matter.

Once overwhelmed by such an abundance of information, many become driven by an excessive determination of finding the one and only truth. After having spent so much time being brain stormed by the Web, they now stand assured to detain the only full rightness. And who are we to question the validity of this new dogma? How can the opinion of a friendly neighbour or a trusted relative outsmart all this virtual wisdom?

No wonder so many end-up painting themselves into the corner of extremism. This is another proof that too much of anything can be just as bad as not enough of it. At the end of the day, like at the end of this story, it all boils down to gut feeling. So I focus on keeping my gut in shape with my eyes on the ball while I conclude this other original tale that came out of the blue.

Blue Moon

It never occurred to Thomas that it may be so. From his vantage observation seat, he was privileged to attend a new play every day. A lot of the performers were regulars on this set, so Thomas knew most of them by name and had even met many. But don't get me wrong, all he had time for was trading a few words.

'Blue Moon' is the reserved area where Thomas and his wife Linda have a front row, unobstructed view on all the action. Along with them in their loge they usually have three employees. Their little team of five has served a record number of 358 meals in one day. People come from out of town to treat themselves with the original Hong Kong menu cooked at 'Blue Moon'.

Having been on site for twenty-one years, their business has grown and they had to move twice in the same building to have more space. Their current location in the middle of the Fairview Food Court gives them prime visibility and an excellent perspective on the overall dining area. This is the main shopping mall in the West Island area of Montreal. Shoppers start looking for food as early as 11am and Blue Moon serves them until 8pm. A rush challenges the small team at lunch and dinner but they surely do not envy some of the too quiet fast-food counters close to them.

Linda and Thomas migrated from China thirty years ago. They already had relatives living here and were able to join them to work in their Chinatown restaurant. An uncle backed them to sign their first lease at the new Fairview Mall. Working seven days a week for all these years, they still managed to raise three smart sons. Mornings were always precious family time. This is when important dialogue, manners and love were conveyed. A Chinese nanny was taking over while Linda and Thomas were performing from 10am to 8pm. They retired recently and sold their business. Thomas marvels at all this free time he can now manage to his liking. He is impressed to be greeted so happily, wherever he goes, by former performers in the play of his 'Blue Moon' life.

Home Run

There was a quiet group of campers nearby. Suddenly they heard a loud bang and they all froze. What was that? With so much camp fire and propane tanks around, everyone got worried. Was this the first of more explosions to come? George made sure his wife and two kids were safe close to their tent. Gloria got worried sick to not see Fred their thirteen-year-old son. She sent George to look for him. He had left just after dinner to play softball with other campers. George went to see Oliver, the father of John. He is also 13 and hangs out with Fred all the time. Oliver was also worried and joined George to search for his son.

As they approached the softball field, they noticed the game was stopped and a crowd had gathered in the back of left field. Worried that somebody was hurt, both fathers ran to join the commotion. Someone was yelling but most people were congratulating Fred. Bases were loaded and Fred had just hit a home run that made his team win the eighth inning.

Berth was fuming and yelling. It was the third time this year that his site was hit. He loved softball so much that he always insisted on staying on a site with an unobstructed view on the game. He never misses a game, geared with his softball mitt on his left hand and a cold beer in the other. Fred was not a talented batter and already had two strikes. So Berth turned his back to the game just long enough to turn the steaks. This third ball was hit with so much power it luckily missed Berth but capsized his barbecue and made it blow up. Luckily it tumbled into the adjacent river and did not burn anything else. Fish downstream had T-Bone steaks for dinner and George invited Berth and his family for dinner to celebrate Fred's winning home run.

Easy Rider

With winter around the corner, autumn is rushing its way through our days. Children have fun imagining that the clouds look like wild beasts gathering for Halloween.

A spider had an interesting summer, undisturbed between a pine and a maple tree. The backyard of the house in Montreal, Quebec she had selected was surrounded by cedar edges, loaded with an unlimited supply of flying insects. Her vantage location sent hundreds of mosquitoes in her web. She got so big and fat that a large male raven spotted her. Getting ready for his trip down south, he checked the spider every day, waiting for the right time. When the wind and freezing rain announced possible snow, the raven dove to go eat the spider. But the spider had also grown wiser and had built a warning surveillance web. When the raven flew through it, the spider quickly side stepped. The raven missed his target but the spider grabbed the raven's wing and jumped on the raven's back.

Riding the raven like Avatar, the spider was later spotted flying over Philadelphia, due south to the favourite winter retreat for ravens in the warm Florida Keys.

Refuse

We all need food and liquids to survive. But being able to eliminate what we ingest is almost as important. So much so that being deprived of them was an efficient means of torture in war movies when prisoners were forced to repeatedly soil themselves. Almost the same phenomenon applies to trash. New York and other large cities became quickly so ugly and stinky when garbage men went on strike.

Some cities have implemented a smart way to avoid this problem. On each sidewalk of a Barcelona's downtown city block, pleasantly designed structures were added in year 2000. Like sculptured statues they blend-in with many other fancy details like the elaborate street light fixtures. These tube-shaped monuments stand side-by-side, each with a small door on the front, feeding a powerful vacuum conduit intake system. Door # 1 is labelled organic and features the drawing of a banana peel. Door # 2 is labelled recycling with a picture of a plastic water bottle. Door # 3 is labelled trash with the pictogram of an old sneaker on it. Many buildings have added the system. Office and apartment buildings now have it indoors. Garbage trucks are now a rare sight downtown. A state of the art processing plant located 10 km away optimizes the value of all this material.

A new retirement housing project is being conceived to use the technology. On the kitchen counter of each of the 60 apartments lay three flat doors. The three twelve-inch conduit pipes underneath vacuum-suck refuse to equipment located in the basement. Organic trash goes to an industrial compactor. In less than a week, compost comes out of the other end, bagged and ready for resale. Recycled bottles, cans and paper go to bins, separate from other trash that is compacted. Dollies and a small electric tractor are used to haul them out on garbage pick-up days. The sale of compost pays for the salary of two employees sharing the operations so that it is manned every day of the week. Residents no longer have to carry smelly leaking trash in corridors and elevators. Our ancestors have valued the benefit of having drinking water from a tap in the kitchen and use drains to flush the toilet. The same now goes to dispose of trash, efficiently and almost pleasantly.

Donald

It is a known fact that if you repeat a lie often enough, people will start believing that what you say is true. Determined to always win, Donald has learned at a young age that attack is the best defence. Perceived as a handsome businessman, bankers trusted him and financed many high-rise buildings and hotels promoted by Donald. His name was so prominent that it was used as a brand on consumables as diverse as clothing and mattresses. His hunger for wealth seemed limitless.

Then one day his bubble burst. He owed close to a billion dollars when bankers pulled the plug. He was going down the drain big time. But he did not because they felt he was too big a flush. Pushing him to bankruptcy would have been such a drawback for him and his bankers that he fought with all he had. Bullying is another of his inner assets that he added to loads of lies and attacks even on his creditors. He made such an impression that they figured they stood a better chance with him in leash that having him on the loose.

Not being bankrupt, he became just another businessman who sadly lost money while investing in real estate. As such, rules of the Internal Revenue Service allowed him to amortize his investment losses over future gains. Added to his other tricks of the trade, this billion dollars of tax-free earnings, sprung his ego to the utmost level. Now convinced that he was the smartest of all, he became a Republican candidate. Shaded by Donald's charisma, other party celebrities fell one after the other. Partisans cranked-up to win at all cost elected Donald as a chief that could crush any opponent.

The Republican Party felt it lost the last election because their opponents had made a better use of mass media. Determined not to make the same mistake again, they even dug into the Democrats emails to identify reprehensible conduct and blast them with it. Donald is now a finalist to become President of the United States of America. Truth, Respect and Compassion now have a difficult ride uphill to offset this widely viewed rise to the top of a bully who lies and disrespects anyone in his way.

Kind humans must be more prolific before bullies proudly enslave ManKind!

Opportunity

Long ago, in a seminar, I learned that behind most problems possibly hides an opportunity. It was probably in one of the many sales training sessions that I attended. Giving this concept a try, I was impressed at how efficient it is. The main skill it required was to listen to what people say and have an open mind. But this is hard for salespeople who talk so much that you can barely put a word in, even while they pause to breathe. We were trained to formulate open-ended questions so that the customer could better define the need and give you hints, essential to offer the proper solution. Conditioned by these skills, I had to hold myself back from problems seeking. Easy sales still exist and are rewarded equally. But as most competitors go after the easy ones, prices come down as do reduced commission to the salesperson on such transactions.

Perseverance was the other ally. Once I was convinced that I had found a good solution, refusal to my original offer was only material to help me refine my proposal. Most products are mass-produced to satisfy as many users as possible. Such was the case for a four-foot fluorescent lighting fixture I had to sell.

The manufacturer I represented made a wide array of portable lighting fixtures for industrial maintenance applications. Air Canada Airlines already used many of their products for airplane interior maintenance. Every year I would meet their hangar manager to show him new products and listen to his needs. This time he took me inside a Boeing 747 being serviced and asked what self-standing temporary lighting I could offer. It had to run cool so no heat would increase the already warm ambient air of the hangar in the summer. Nothing could be hung-up from the ceiling so it had to be free-standing in a small footprint area in the aisle between seats. The light output had to be strong but not distort the jacket colour of each conductor being spliced.

Not being sure I had such a product, I spent the next two evenings in my basement workshop modifying a sample. It was made to be hung-up horizontally from pipes or other beams on a construction site. A heavy-duty clear Lexan four-inch tube, four feet long was its lens and dispersed ample lighting over 360 degrees around it. I noticed that its 4" clear Lexan lens could fit inside a standard 4" toilet base flange. Once secured to a 24" diameter, ¾" plywood, it could remain upright as a stand-alone. This was much less floor space than what alternative tripods required.

Air Canada liked my solution and most airlines have also adopted it. This manufacturer used it as an example to train new staff on how to turn a problem in an opportunity like this one that became their most profitable product for a few years in a row.

Skipping

I looked at the water and wondered what I should do. After a while I figured flat stones' skipping on the surface was the way to go. But how fast must I go to stay afloat I wondered. Surely it required great speed. But once attained how to maintain the momentum? Using the wind was the solution. It blew in the correct direction so I used my pop-tent as a parasail. Testing it for a few minutes on the beach confirmed it could work. I could barely hold it back while I walked as far away from the shore and figured I had to try it before sundown.

My camping trip on Dawker Island had started so well. The weather had been perfect for my canoe trip across from Beaconsfield. Exploring the island, I found a clearing and settled in what felt like paradise. The island is uninhabited but many boaters use its protected bay for mooring. Crickets sang wildly most of the night and kept me sound asleep. It was only 5:30am when the circus arrived. At least that is how it sounded. Sunrise had just initiated the process and on cue, all performers sounded like they were setting-up for an outstanding show. I had to see what was going on so I unzipped the tent and peaked out. All of a sudden, I thought I was camping inside the Montreal Biosphere. Hundreds of birds of all shape and sizes were singing and jetting by in frenzy.

By the time I got dressed and out of the tent, I understood what caused the turmoil. A hurricane strong wind storm came out of nowhere and blew my tent and all my belongings out on the lake. Luckily my tent got stuck in branches and stayed. But my canoe had vanished from the shore and no boater was left on the lake.

Not a good enough swimmer, I elected to make the most of the freak wind and my left over tent shreds. Backed-up the little slope off the tree line, I stood with the tent fully blown and started to run towards the lake. Using the flat part of my heels like skipping stones, I counted steps and was amazed to skip so well. But after skip number 28, the water was up to my ankles. About to drown, soggy to say the least, I woke-up glad to be in my bed at home.

Seated

"Please wait to be seated," said the sign. My wife and I barely had the time to notice it when we were greeted by "Good Morning love birds. I was expecting you and saved a good table for your breakfast. Will you come this way, please?" At first we thought her greeting was excessive but with the broad smile and languorous southern drawl of Michelle, we played along as new characters in her show. Most tables could sit four or more people. She suggested that we sit side-by-side to share the same view outside the hotel. We complied and once seated, noticed that the other twenty patrons that were in pairs were also sitting elbow to elbow.

While we were looking at the menu, Michelle left us, already intoning a new introduction hymn as she said, "Welcome Honey, it's so nice to see you again this morning. I was hoping you would come so, I saved this table just for you." This business lady, hauling a fancy briefcase on wheels gave her an icy look. There again Michelle's persistent smile melted all restraints, and the lady joined the act. A bit reluctant at first to sit next to another business woman, she complied, having no time to lose.

We all were under her spell and admired her way of serving coffee and anticipating each client's needs. A pleasant murmur emerged from each table as everyone's closeness only required whispers to converse. It was such a pleasant sight that my wife and I switched to the other side of our table to view Michelle's masterpiece play instead of outside pedestrians' traffic.

Excellent service was her ultimate goal. As she tended to each table, she made sure we remembered to tell her when we wanted more coffee or water. Did we want to take along an apple or a banana for our morning break? She offered advice to first-time visitors in Savannah and gave a small bottle of water to tourists out for a stroll through town. Michelle's performance was remarkable. She made us all forget the $10 charge for continental breakfast that is usually complimentary in other hotels. Most customers left her company so pleased that we noticed she was being tipped generously. We will always remember how much we looked forward to being seated by Michelle on each of our three mornings in Savannah, Georgia.

Floaters

Albert was the fourth to join the Pool Meeting. He had played golf all morning with the men's team. A total of six foursomes met for lunch at the Blue Heron Lounge. While having a drink they recorded their scores. Only two players did better than his 92, so he was happy to be back with a decent score amongst his Florida golfing group. A little later, as Albert was walking down the steps into the pool, Shawn asked him, "How was your game?" "My back nine was a mess but so it was for most golfers, so I finished amongst the best" replied Albert.

The kidney-shaped outdoor pool on Oak Cove Road is fully screened and could safely hold no more than twenty adults. The hot tub next to it can sit eight and is busy at all hours, day and night. Another pool in the resort is much larger and can handle about one hundred. Albert prefers this smaller pool. Located only a five minutes' walk from his house he is always sure to find in it a few friendly neighbours ready for a chat. Today's Pool Meeting was attended by Reba, Teresa and Cindy. They were discussing a recipe that Loretta was famous for. Her zucchini pie was such a favourite that they will help her make ten of them for Thanksgiving.

It is amazing to see how seriously the American people celebrate this holiday. The fact that it is not related to one religion in particular probably helps. Stores and the media stir consumers' frenzy to full intensity. Roads and airports overflow with travellers all driven by family reunions. Albert and his wife decided to celebrate with friends instead. The resort's Interdenominational Christian Church gathers fine people from all over. The Church Thanksgiving Dinner serves two-hundred meals of turkey and ham. But locals happily bring a dish to share, along with their own table cutlery.

What a funny and friendly sight it is to see them, in the pool, planning that meal. Even Shawn who is heavily handicapped and can barely move with his walker is now bobbing about supported by two 5 feet long foam noodles under his arms to stay afloat, like others in the pool. Their meeting ended and ten of these happy floaters have agreed to share a table at the Church Thanksgiving dinner and rightfully name it the "Pool Table".

Majestic Stanley

When money is no object, what do people do? Most will buy things, travel and give a little to the poor. Supporting their children and relatives from one or many marriages will add-up to considerable amounts. Cumulating paintings, cars, furniture and fitness equipment will require a larger house and land to match this wealth and social standing. Passion will get many to acquire enough collectibles to start a museum.

Luxurious cruises or private jets will let them visit or stay in the most prestigious resorts or villas anywhere, for as long as they want. So much wealth will open doors for them at the most private clubs where they will be introduced to local politicians and business people. Linked to most artistic activities of the area, a private tour of artists' studios will be made possible. This is where they will order a special work of art made especially for them, matching an elaborate décor in the foyer of their mansion or pool in their garden atrium. Exquisite art galleries will make sure they are invited to jet-set vernissages. Complex and sturdy crates will be custom-built, like this one, protecting a very delicate crystal chandelier.

Such a huge candelabra was built for Stanley Jones over a period of eight months in Murano shops near Venice, Italy. It was twelve feet in diameter and twenty feet high. The protective shipping crate itself cost a fortune and its transportation, even more. The ocean crossing from Venice to Miami, Florida took another month. It arrived in Durham, Florida, its final destination, just in time for the opening. A crew of specialists came from Italy to install the chandelier and, it became the 'pièce de résistance' in the gigantic foyer of the new Jones Hotel. On the opening day of April 30th 1930, all of the privately invited distinguished guests came from all over the world to admire this masterpiece and attend the Hotel's inauguration ball. The two hundred luxury suites were all occupied by privileged invitees. They marvelled at being the first to use these facilities including the Olympic size indoor pool and huge Turkish bath for fifty people.

The Jones Hotel remained a must vacationing destination for the rich and famous during the following thirty years. But when in 1960 Stanley Jones was diagnosed with a rare incurable disease and, short of a smart enough heir to run his hotel, he donated it to the Town of Durham. The Town Council could not support the cost of heavy repair and upgrade required to meet modern safety codes for hotels. The construction of a new City Hall had been postponed for many years due to a shortage of funds. Studies showed that the hotel building could be converted to office space at minimal cost. Town Hall moved in and now rents the extra space to local professionals, proud to have such a prestigious address. This is how it still stands today, along with its magnificent tropical garden courtyard. Most weddings of this county come here for pictures or the whole ceremony.

The annexed four storey sports complex was going to be demolished. Only months before the deadline, Jack Lightstrong's salvation proposal was accepted. His own family's heritage was considerable but not enough to support this project alone. Still, his commitment to seventy percent of the budget, convinced fifteen other investors to join his venture. Renovation work started in 1968 with the conversion of the Olympic pool into a prestigious ballroom surrounded by three storeys of arched balconies. An army of cabinetmakers restored the wonderful woodwork and the exotic hardwood floors were rejuvenated.

Jack had collected an impressive array of artwork over the years. Short of space in his huge oceanfront Florida mansion, he had most of it on loan to museums all over the world. September 1st, 1969 is when he inaugurated his Lightstrong Art Museum. It still stands today as an example of outstanding beauty. The building itself is worth the visit to admire its unique architecture. Other art collectors recognized the magic of this perfect set-up and prided themselves to have their valuables advantageously displayed in such a lovely setting. Visitors cannot help but share the passion of enthusiastic volunteers who guide them to point out the master craft and origin of each majestic item.

This Majestic Stanley story is fiction inspired by the visit of the beautiful:
Lightner Museum located at
75 King Street, Saint Augustine, Florida 32084

Sorrow Bin

Could have, should have, would have, and other similar marks of doubt and deception all go to my sorrow bin. This way I keep them out of my way to an active and happy life. The bin is conveniently located behind my left shoulder. Discretely I can use my right hand to dump into it while I pretend to scratch. Caution is required to monitor pressure build-up in it and allow some steam to be released occasionally. Unless you empty it regularly, you need a large enough bin to avoid overflow but it may be heavier to carry. Some 'IFs' and a few 'BUTs' must be allowed to surface during an unbearable period for decision-making. For me, this phase is hectic and crucial to minimize the possible emergence of future regrets.

Knowing that the world should easily outlast my own passage in it, my main challenge is to make today and tomorrow more enjoyable than yesterday. Of course, some days in my past were filled with enough joy difficult to replicate. Perception is what counts and it differs immensely from each individual's perspective. Paying attention to details, while being receptive to beauty, makes every moment special. Focus on that can be tricky; too close to the trees limits admiring the forest. The same stands for people around us. I noticed that a harmonious way of being is what I perceive as most pleasant in others. None of us has had much saying in our innate physical attributes. Yet, some of the most likeable people I know have such a radiant attitude that it obliterates any physical imperfection they may have.

The fascinating emergence of a new day must not be taken lightly. It affects and regulates humanity from as far as its origin. Like the teacher who erases the class blackboard at the end of the day, I like to start the new day facing a clean slate. Most of mine start at 6:30am with a white page lit by a lamp. Not long after, natural light takes over and refills my willpower reserve. Inspiration to write overflows while I give it all my attention and I rapidly fill a new page. People and nature around me get intertwined into events that I elect to lead towards a positive outcome. Of course problems show up and dent the outer layer of my attitude. This is where years of determined preference for joy, leaves my soul with mere scratches that a little love quickly brings back to full shine.

Awaken

When I awaken this morning, it was not clear if I was in my own bed or not. It was pitch dark, so I figured it must be very cloudy outside. The 648 digits on the alarm clock only spew a bleak glow. It sure was not enough light to see details of the room and all I could hear was my wife's heavy breathing, on my left. So I elected to stay in bed trying to sleep a little longer but in vain.

The night had been somewhat exciting. First I was cross-country skiing in Rawdon. I enjoyed the glide on a trail lined with icicle frilled giant pine trees. My mind shifted movie channels just before the trail ended in the waterfall. Cocoa Beach Florida is where I snoozed next. I ducked just in time to avoid the Frisbee that kids were throwing on the beach. Sylvie and I walked the broad sandy beach for an hour. When we got to the pier, cool Margaritas hit the spot just in time.

As we sat at the bar, Dundee came to sit next to us. His wild Australian accent made us chat with him. Distance not being important, we joined him on his kangaroo farm. All was well until he showed us our bedroom in his guests' room, above the garage. Strangely, my wife was already in bed but on the wrong side of the bed which was so awkward that I woke up, reassuringly in my bed.

Fear

He could feel that something was bound to happen but he could not figure out what or when. As early as five on Monday morning, Philip sat straight-up in his bed, so stunned that he was scared to stay in bed any longer. He busied himself making coffee and reading the morning paper delivered to his door soon after he awoke. His good healthy breakfast put his mind at rest. He attended his usual Monday morning aquacise session and other planned activities. At the end of the day, he was mighty glad he had made it without a hitch.

Philip's wife had died four years before. They had a lot of friends, all very supportive of one another. He needed them to make another transition this year, as they finally convinced him to retire at age 67. Except for some occasional arthritis pain, he felt fairly fit. He often joined friends skiing, cycling, golfing or playing some tennis. But since Monday morning, he felt like a strained dog walking sideways, afraid of being kicked from behind.

Tuesday afternoon is when he preferred to buy groceries every week. He figured he could go at 2pm once he got his doctor's appointment confirmed. After lunch he called his doctor's office to set a date for his annual check-up. When he finally got to speak to someone, not just a machine, the secretary was sad to inform him that his doctor had passed away last month. No replacement family doctor had accepted to replace him yet, so Philip was given a list of other doctors he could contact. He spent the balance of his day at this and, ultimately found one he could see in two weeks.

The Wednesday morning crowd at the grocery store was very different than his usual Tuesday acquaintances. Busy following and checking-off items on his list, he did not pay much attention to other shoppers. They all looked unfamiliar until he spotted her close to the end of the bread section. The woman was looking so much like his deceased wife, he just about fainted. People in the aisle noticed he was troubled and supported him when he nearly collapsed.

Noticing the commotion and being a nurse, she offered to help. When she recognized him, she confirmed to Philip that she was not a ghost but his wife's twin sister, Rosanne, whom he had not seen for the past thirty years. Ever since they were teenagers, the two sisters could not help but fight when they met. Their last encounter ended in a cat fight with broken dishes and a few bruises. Philip had tried to reconcile them but had to let the matter go in support of his wife. Rosanne had never married but had recently retired from the head nurse position that had occupied most of her life.

Rosanne and Philip can now be seen every Wednesday filling a mutual grocery cart. Philip willfully changed his shopping day to be with her more. They became best friends always available to alleviate each other's fear of growing old alone.

Merry

Christmas in Florida is a peculiar snowbird experience. Like anywhere else in America, decorations become a contest. Houses are often landscaped with artificial snow and other references to a white Xmas. Strangely enough, many Christmas Floridians come here to avoid shovelling snow and scraping icy windshields. Yet, Santa can be seen approaching a lot of houses in his snow sled and lighted icicles hang from eavestroughs all around most houses.

In trying to differentiate themselves from neighbours, people take Christmas to a stratospheric level. Giant inflatable and lighted Santas can be seen driving a lawnmower, a bulldozer or flying a rocket. Reindeers become dinosaurs or various Disney cartoon stars. Xmas lights have become automated light shows supported by digital music. Walking along such streets is like going to a TV store with twenty TV screen each showing a different channel while sound systems in the next row add to the cacophonic ambiance.

This is sad, considering that every household has dedicated an important amount of effort and money to fit the street's décor. One's assessment can be that such excess is just as bad as a shortage. Laser light projectors looked like a good idea when introduced a few years ago. From a single compact source, they sprinkle millions of coloured lighted dots, moving all over your house. But people forget that laser beams travel over long distances and even become a weapon that can blind airplane pilots or a neighbour driving by.

After a few days of immersion in this euphoria, people change. An exchange of "Merry Christmas" wishes are traded with strangers who no longer ignore each other. Everyone gets busy adding magic to Christmas Eve or Christmas Day. We are unable to replicate in Florida the thirty family members' reunions that we have experienced in our youth. So, we elected to visit the kingdom of magic at Disney. Being surrounded by Merry people in awe of wonderful, more traditional Christmas decorations and music, make our stay at the Grand Floridian Hotel pleasantly meet our expectations for our Christmas to be Merry.

Resolution

With the start of this New Year, Rick instinctively thought of the necessity for identifying his resolutions. It has been so every year for as long as he can remember. His parents and later his teachers at school prompted the process and encouraged its accomplishment. Judy went through similar stages and, once married to Rick, perpetuated this fine tradition with their three children.

Now approaching their seventies, Judy and Rick had tackled most challenging necessities through nearly fifty years of marriage. Determined to live healthily and fit many more years, they rarely drank alcohol and had stopped smoking thirty years ago. So these two difficult resolutions were not on their list. Retirement had slightly shaken the stability of their household. Judy retired from work two years before Rick. His resolution on Judy's second year of retirement was to no longer expect dinner on the table when he returned from work. It took him a while but he finally accepted that Judy had retired to enjoy her free time, not to become his maid. But when Rick retired and started enjoying this lovely house of theirs, Judy was often upset to no longer have the whole house to herself all day. As usual, their love and experienced ability to compromise, allowed this New Year to flow downstream gently.

Like previous years, they had initiated the discussion of acceptable resolutions at the beginning of December. Various chores were discussed but found too superficial to be considered seriously. They did make a point to challenge themselves by writing down each New Year's resolution commitments. They called it their ship's log book and it was fun to read and recall each resolution recorded since January 1980 when they started. It is Judy who found the one for year 2017 as she was looking in their lobby's mirror while settling her hat on her way outside. Not liking her own reflection, she fixed it instantly with a smile so it could also influence others. This is how the 2017 resolution for both Judy and Rick officially became: to always greet others with an inviting smile in hope that it will be mirrored in return by others.

Flowing Motion

With the start of a new season, Remy was determined to train in order to improve his bowling score. Not long ago, one would have had to wander through many libraries to find training books or pay trainers for lessons. Nowadays, YouTube offers a lot of that at your fingertips. At his convenience, any time of day, Remy can go online and watch training videos made by professionals. Each with a slightly different approach, Remy was not experienced enough to identify the best ones so, he started watching them as they flow one after another on his computer.

There are so many that he wondered if they were endless. Each video varies in duration and gives valid improvement information. Most lead to advertise another website where, for a membership fee, you can get a more complete training program. As a neophyte in this game, Remy viewed about thirty videos in a week. Keeping notes about the ones he preferred, he viewed them again while practicing in his basement exercise room. He had underestimated the complexity of this sport. The footsteps were just as important as in Tango dancing. Starting with the wrong foot throws you off balance right from the start. He tried to remember each detail and link them into a harmonious motion leading to a precise throw every time.

To avoid rushing at the last minute, he arrived thirty minutes in advance. Remy was surprised to see the place already crowded with enthusiasts. Most of them had not seen each other since the end of last season, nine months ago. All were smiling, glad to be amongst so many happy people and exchange news with team players. After a welcoming speech by the manager and a few practice throws, Remy was chosen to be the first to start. Eager to apply all his newly acquired wisdom, he soon had to admit that he would need much more practice. Dwane, his team leader, told Remy to fall back on his own style after he did so poorly in the first game. That changed his next game radically and he scored one hundred points more than in his first game. His third and last game was just as good and helped his team attain the best average score of all teams for their first afternoon of bowling together in 2017.

Dozing

Alex was becoming a hazard when driving his car alone. He would doze off unexpectedly while driving and many times woke up just in time to avoid an accident. Frightening moments were only compensated by his excellent reflexes and driving skills. He also had a good sense of direction so, he never got lost. This was essential for his line of work. As a sales representative for industrial supplies, he had to visit customers all over a very large territory. His problem mostly occurred after lunch or driving back home at the end of the day. Long distances also triggered the process. But he had to drive them in order to present samples and catalogues to prospect users in remote areas. He drove for an average of three hours per day, but his farthest customers were twelve hours away. Most times he could break the journey over a few days but twice he had to stay awake for these boring long hours in one stretch.

He did well enough that Alex was able to retire before he was sixty. His wife Melanie had retired a few years before and welcomed her partner in her new life. They had travelled the world over the years but now felt the urge to spend winter away from the cold. They elected to buy a small property in a Florida resort. This gated community of about two thousand residents is surrounded by wilderness but only a ten minute drive away from stores and restaurants. So once on the resort's 15 mph speed controlled roads, risk of falling asleep behind the wheel was less fatal. Getting there was the challenge. A total of twenty-five hours of driving each way became a nightmare. Melanie was no help in keeping Alex awake because she too was dozing off even more.

Flying was the solution adopted by many snowbirds. Some would have a used car on site on their Florida lot. Alex found it excessively costly considering the minimal use of this car once on site. 'AutoTrain' is a fun alternative. Its Superliner Bedroom with in-room toilet and shower make it a magic way to shave away fifteen endless hours on interstates. All aboard is done close to Washington, DC at 2:30pm and you arrive close to Orlando, FL at 10:30am the next day. Dinner and breakfast are served in the luxurious Dining Car. An evening walk through the train can also let you enjoy the Lounge Car. All this while your own car is also resting on this same train. Once in Orlando, Alex only had an hour's drive to get to his paradise winter retreat. Melanie liked this option that allowed her to bring along in the car, many items too costly to fly.

But next year they may use a completely different concept. 'Car2Go' now offered another simple and cost-efficient solution. Their resort's community was large enough to keep two shared cars on the resort. Alex and Melanie would fly to Florida and go online to reserve a car for a day or only a few hours. Now standing as experienced snowbirds, very few items have to be transferred south with them. Their car could stay home in Canada and last longer without all this useless mileage. The little 'Car2Go' rental car is enough to do most errands or spend the day on the beach. All other moves are made walking or cycling through their dreamland resort and have the great benefit of keeping them alive, in shape and awake.

Road Side

And so it was, after he felt that all was said and done, that it really started. All would be different from that point on. He envisioned this day for so long that he was living it as a daydreaming robot, almost watching himself from the outside. The view from his window seat flying over the clouds of the Pacific Ocean enhanced his transition.

Mario was now forty-two years old and free as a bird. He got married when he was twenty but it lasted only three years. His parents ran a small taxi business in Verdun, Quebec. Mario completed his college education but started driving a taxi as a student. He liked it more than studying theories; he preferred his thrilling exposure to real people and their so varied life styles.

For the past five years, Mario was pretty much running the business on his own. His parents always enjoyed trout fishing and were progressively retiring. With thousands of lakes and rivers not accessible by road in Quebec, his father learned to fly and bought a small seaplane. When the weather was right, they would fly away for a few days, assured that Mario would run things smoothly in their absence.

The construction industry in Quebec shuts down job sites for the last two weeks of July. This sends thousands of workers on forced vacation. While a lot of these people are out of town, the taxi business slows down significantly. So Mario's parents took advantage of this period to fly away for at least one week to fish in pristine rivers in farther areas of northern Quebec. Using a satellite phone, they kept Mario aware of their whereabouts every second day or so.

He had been busy dealing with employees menacing to strike and did not worry on the third day. But after four days of silent phone, he advised authorities and a rescue search started. Close to the shore of Tast Lake and the mouth of Broadback River, rescuers spotted their plane with only the tail sticking out of the water. The glare from the sun had probably hidden a large boulder just below the surface. It capsized their plane on the landing. The shock was so sudden their necks probably snapped and they drowned helplessly in their seats, in ten feet of water passed the boulder. Mario was so affected by the tragedy that he sold the business a month later.

He had met Miko, a lovely Japanese girl while attending a taxi convention in Chicago the year before. She was sitting across from him at a table of eight. They were part of a discussion group about the taxi new dispatching systems. He could not keep his eyes off her and she found him funny with a beatific kind of smile stuck to his face. She accepted his invitation to dinner, and they spent all their free time together in Chicago. They both were astonished to hear how similar their individual life stories had been.

Through emails and Skype they kept in contact at least once a week. Mario was fascinated by her life in Tokyo and Miko invited him to come and work with her since he knew the business so well. Once he accepted, Mario visited all his friends and relatives one last time before his departure. He made sure all his paperwork was in order after the sale of his house, as he did with most of his belongings.

Feeling reborn, Mario was fascinated by the prospect of living in a city like Tokyo, different from Montreal in so many ways. He had started lessons in Japanese and was now able to read and write it fairly well. But the one thing he was most eager to experience was to be driving in Japan, on the wrong side of the road.

Has Been

All of us have had a very active life. The most persevering have completed a university degree but we all have had to eventually look for a job. The luckiest has worked in a domain with advancement. Through consistent good work ethics, some were promoted to interesting positions. Meanwhile we have raised families with a similar set of values.

Spanned over an average of more than forty years, our most active part of life is often perceived as a rat race. Your survival is always dependent on your ability to perform. A known replacement is always on standby if you are disabled for too long. Time slowly but surely takes its hold on your own frame but, like others, you endure and hope to make it to retirement in good shape.

At first, the emptiness hits you below the belt. Having seen others go through the process, you had a vague idea of what it's like to have an agenda with so many blank pages. With the help of friends and relatives, you try sports and social activities that you never had time for. A few months later you discover that you are committed to do so many activities that you must consult your agenda a few times a day. Through the process, you notice that a lot of your neighbours are on a similar schedule. You meet them in your Tai-Chi class or in the town pool for the aquacise session. But it is at your local grocery store that you really get acquainted. You stop and chat for a few minutes and you are astonished to find out that you have been living a block away from each other.

This same phenomenon happens with others at the library or the pharmacy during the day. You make new friends who actually have been living close to you for more than ten years. Like you, they were so loaded with responsibilities that they never took time to befriend neighbours who looked just as busy. Now liberated from the daily hustle and bustle, you can make the most out of daylight and sunlight. You avoid rushing errands on icy and heavy rain days. The question no longer is 'to be or not to be' because a 'has been' is way too busy 'fully being'.

Travelling Spirit

Max could hardly stay in bed all night. One dream followed another giving him a preview of his next day. He made it out of bed early and at 7am he was already on his Harley cruising by South Beach in Miami to watch the sunrise out of the ocean. The good weather forecast and the sparkling blue sky, with a rare cloud or two made it a perfect riding day. So Max headed south towards the Florida Keys. He wended his way using many side roads to find remote beaches. By the end of the day he had made it to Key West and stayed there touring the area for a week.

His next trip was on a seaplane. Max had always dreamed of owning a model with at least one thousand miles of autonomy. He now could afford it and planned a long adventure across America. For weeks, he prepared for it by making sure he would fly to each region during its best weather period. Using all main landmarks like the Grand Canyon as targets, he mapped his flight pattern through many states. All major cities were also to be visited and required special permits from federal authorities. Some lakes and rivers are forbidden to seaplanes so he selected resorts or hotels near an acceptable waterway with a marina that could accommodate him.

He was so passionate about his virtual reality helmet that he often yelled at his nurses when they removed it from his head. Clara was his wife and like him was an Olympic downhill ski champion. She had met Max at a ski training camp in Colorado. On a joy ride in their small sports car, Clara died on the spot when a drunk, driving through a red traffic light, hit her side of the car.

Max came out of a coma two weeks later paralyzed from the neck down. Clara was the love of his life so he just wanted to die. Technology saved him for now. This new full head helmet is activated by his eyes and lips only. He can now virtually see and hear so much. He can even see himself live limitless adventures all over the world. He thinks it is almost as good as being there. Max does not have the choice but if he had, he would immediately trade this helmet link to virtual fun for a minute more of the real Clara.

Skilled

The saying 'Winning is Everything' is highly overrated. Of course there will always be winners and losers. And anyone with lesser abilities may be rejected by peers. Competing is a necessary evil to help fund sports activities. And each of us carries an inner beast that is driven to dominate a certain amount of space in order to survive. Romans surely optimized the concept in the arena where gladiators had to fight to defeat other beasts, human or not.

All he ever wanted was to be able to play and belong to a team. But John was gifted. He always excelled in every sport he tried. Even schooling became a game for him. His photographic memory astonished his teachers who could not help but give him an A-plus repeatedly. His parents were both career professionals and luckily were aware of the possible downside of such overwhelming talent. They made sure that John understood his responsibility to make the most of his extraordinary wits. He also realized the danger of constantly riding the crest of a wave and he prepared himself for when it eventually faded away.

Some of the sports he preferred were extreme. He had fractured his right elbow when he fell on landing from a ski jump. His two legs were scarred from bicycle crashes while racing. His parents attended most of his important games and one day, ran short of walls and shelves to display his numerous winning medals and trophies. John also liked to read biographies of his favourite sports stars. It helped guiding his long-term perspective and made him realize the heavy burden his body had to endure in maintaining this high level of performance. Most athletes start suffering from constant pain in their mid-forties. Pain killers become a necessity to compensate for the abuse they imposed on most of their body's joints for so long.

John chose a career in dentistry. After only a few years of practice, he was already reputed to be excellent, particularly with children and retirees. He devoted his free time to his family but also coached hockey in winter and football in summer. His relatives and friends were always happy to see him for he has mastered his preferred skill which remains to simply 'belong'.

Should Have

It is always a matter of choice, thought Rick. He hates having to regret a decision. So he avoids saying "I should have" and when he does, he turns the occasion into a fun exploratory journey.

Spur of the moment decisions are unavoidable. Rick found a way to have some control over these also. In his free time, he envisaged various happenings. This gave him time to debate what direction would best suit him. Sometimes, many years later, that very situation repeated itself and Rick whisked his way through it with a feeling of "déjà vu".

This served him well the other day. With his wife Lisa, on their way to the Montreal airport, their taxi driver fainted at the wheel and rear-ended the car ahead. Luckily the traffic was heavy, so the impact was from a short distance and at low speed. Lisa had first-aid skills that saved the driver while Rick called 911 and assisted Lisa. By the time the ambulance got there, and policemen reported the accident, an hour had gone by. They were now running short of time to catch their flight to Orlando. The police officer was kind enough to recognize their help in saving the driver so he drove them to the airport backed by a blaring siren and lots of flashing lights.

The new international flights terminal had just been completed and considerably changed the departure whereabouts. Here again, Rick's exploration habit came very handy. Last month, this new terminal had been in operation for only a week. Rick and Lisa made a dinner reservation at the fine restaurant of the luxury hotel in the terminal. With dinner, parking was free for three hours. So, after an enjoyable and appetizing meal, they ventured through the magnificent new facilities and simulated a departure for Brazil. Having a coffee amongst all these travellers was almost as exciting as leaving with them. In the process, they had also checked where and how to quickly check-in for Orlando, Florida. So as soon as their blazing trooper turned them loose at the curb, they made it through security and to the gate just in time to avoid a "should have".

Canasta Owl

Every year, a tropical storm or two frightens Florida residents. This year, the one called Matthew had hurricane strength and scarred many paradise areas.

Anna Maria Island was one of them. Located an hour's drive south of Tampa, FL, three bridges keep it linked to the coast of the Gulf of Mexico. Northerners of America and Canada have recognized its beautiful beaches so much that today, every possible building space is occupied.

The storm raged through the area for two days. Accustomed residents had prepared to hold the fort against the invader. All lawn patio and BBQ furnishings had been stowed away. Any loose object was at risk of becoming a deadly projectile. Most houses on Canasta Drive had window storm shutters locked tight and ready for the worst.

The weather forecast had seen it coming, so Ralph and Ray followed the warning instructions. They made sure they had all groceries and necessities to avoid leaving the safe shelter of their home during the storm. But they were worried for the safety of the Barn Owl nesting in a giant oak tree across the street. They noticed that the little ones appeared a few days ago and feared for their survival.

Tuesday at noon, the nightmare suddenly stopped. An almost insulting peace was back. Pretending it never was lethal, the wind was now a soothing balm, under a bright blue sky. Ralph could not wait any longer and rushed out to see his owl neighbour. Debris was all over his street, and five little chicks cried loudly in their nest. But the mother was nowhere to be seen. Looking around for where she might be, he found her twenty feet away at the base of a palm tree. Luckily she was still alive but probably knocked out of her nest by one of the many coconuts that the storm had sent airborne.

Gail and her husband Ed run the Wildlife Rehabilitation Center just a block away from there. She was patiently feeding the six turtles presently under treatment in her front yard. Gail jumped when she heard Ralph running towards her shouting. Delicately whisking the owl from his arms, she went straight to the X-ray machine in her lab. It revealed no broken bones and the owl's twisting neck was back in motion a few days later. The large bird was lucky that Ralph had rescued her before predators got to her. Gail phoned a friend with a boom truck and brought the chicks down to be with their mother just before ravens got to them.

A few weeks later, the owl and her chicks were well enough to make it on their own. Many friends came to wish them farewell. All will remember this saved family. Even Gaspar, the large parrot was impressed. He is Gail's alert staff. No one can come close to the clinic without hearing his warning screams. Having witnessed Ralph's salvage of the owl, Gaspar now welcomes Ralph's every visit with a loud "Hello Ralph".

Cicada or Ant

The Cicada or the Ant; which one should I prefer? In the fable of Jean De La Fontaine, the cicada had the pleasant role, having spent most of the summer singing. Whereas it is the more industrious work of the ant that is usually admired. It so happens that both are present in the backyard universe of our house. After a thorough study of their behaviour, here is what I observed.

Earing the singing of the cicada confirms that the temperature will be hot. Often we already know it by the sweat that we profuse even in the shade. Its occasional song is tolerable, almost entertaining and exotic. But I imagine that if a hundred cicadas echoed their serenades, it would become infernal. Between its vocalizations, the cicada feeds on smaller insects, which is excellent especially if it is those who sting us. From the treetops it has a superb view over its kingdom. But it must relocate often because, master raven, attracted by the cicada's song, can now target it as a snack.

An ant always looks busy and on its way somewhere. It helps pollinate the plants by pacing from flower to flower. Of sedentary and familial nature, it is when they regroup by thousands that their presence disturbs. In order to build a protected residence, they dig tunnels in the parterre, visible by the mound of dirt stacked next to it. These engineering works are admirable but disastrous when the lawn is dotted with them. Disrespectful of others' property, it is when they come to lodge in the walls and the cabinets of your house that they disturb the most. This barbaric invasion of my living space is for me an act of war that I urgently repel with insecticide.

Jean de La Fontaine was right to speak of them in the singular form because it is thus that the cicada and the ant are, like humans, the most neighbourly.

Wish-For

Karl has learned long ago to be careful of what he would wish-for because, once he convinced his wife, it was bound to happen. As a plumber he now had four employees and such a good reputation that he earned a decent living. Clara, his wife, had been a teacher for twenty years before she was promoted to be the principal of Courtland Elementary School. Like everyone around them, they worked hard all their lives and could now start reaping some benefits.

Clara's brother and his wife invited them to join their winter vacation in Mexico. In an all-inclusive resort of the Riviera Maya, they could hardly believe they were still on the same planet. Having left dead looking vegetation, stuck in ice and snow the same morning in Courtland, NY they found it excessively unfair on the same day, to be freed of winter clothing and surrounded by lush gardens. Even more so, the resort's promotional flyer stated that this paradisiacal weather was the norm all year round. On the morning of the fifth day, Clara told Karl that she wished to avoid the harshness of New-York State winters at retirement. Courtland was a lovely and safe heaven but the cold temperature was making her arthritis pain worsen every winter for the past five years. With only six more vacation days to go in Mexico, she already noticed she was painless, so Karl shared her wish to retire soon to warm climates, but not sure where.

Luis and Helen had been their neighbors and friends for twelve years. For retirement, they had visited most of Canada, the USA and Mexico aboard a small motorhome. They had sold their Courtland property so they could be free to set a new nest wherever it suited them best. After being on the road for more than 200,000 miles, they elected to set up camp in a Florida resort. After criss-crossing the continent and revisiting their favorite sites, The Great Outdoors Resort in Titusville, FL was their preferred paradise. This RV friendly Golf and Tennis resort of 1,500 property owners is not owned by anybody else. The operation budget is voted by the 1,500 owners, so no one is making a profit over and above. The cost of this quality living is one of the lowest in America. But its level of active-living is way above anywhere else. Free or low-cost activities abound in numerous first-class amenities. Each person is able to join activities at will and soon make friends with loads of like-minded people from all over the world. Luis made sure their set-up was complete on their own lot facing the 10th hole tee-off and, the week after, he joined the fun. He went bowling on Mondays, played tennis on Tuesdays, Wednesdays, Fridays, Saturdays and, roller-skated with Karl on Thursdays. Helen preferred to go to the Tai-Chi class on Mondays, Wednesdays and Fridays, then to aquacise on Tuesdays and Thursdays.

They had kept contact and trusted their friends' judgment, so Karl and Clara did not bother to search other communities. Luis and Helen identified a nice lot close to theirs and Karl and Clara came to see it and bought it while on a short spring break visit. Not being able to use it now, they rented it and covered most of their operating cost. Two years later, Karl and Clara had retired and started playing for a living. Surrounded by palm and pine trees, bottlebrush and azalea flowers, they often walk together on the resort's nature trails abounding with eagles, herons, armadillos, turtles, alligators and so many other creatures lucky enough to live here. So happy with this new life, good health is now all they wish-for.

Hurricane

The Weather Channel says a hurricane is coming our way and, after causing serious damage to Cuba, it now threatens Florida. Many Quebecers have a residence in Florida and are wondering if they should flee or stay. We, like them, follow every move of the storm on specialized weather websites. It is phenomenal to have easy access to all this information. Not only do we see the current situation but also the anticipated position of the hurricane for up to four days ahead.

Florida is preparing for the worst. All objects that are normally left outside are now stored in solid buildings. The wind is so powerful, it turns a chair into a projectile that can break many windows or kill someone. Drains and sewers are cleaned and tested to ensure that they can evacuate the expected massive rainfall. The evacuation roads are repaired and well identified because the distances to reach a safe area are long. People who decide to ride the storm at home, barricade themselves and many plywood boards now cover the shop windows. Grocery stores are quickly emptied as the population accumulates provisions to survive a possible siege of many days against this invader.

During all this time, he remains very quiet and observes the situation. Only a pair of eyes emerges from the surface of the frilled water, but his look betrays a certain anxiety, probably caused by this abnormal hubbub. He noticed the displacement of birds that sensed the imminent danger and evacuated as one big flock. Surprised nevertheless to see that the golfers are more reckless and present themselves anyway for tee-off, at the scheduled departure time. From his pond along the 18th hole, he is well positioned to observe this circus. All alligator that he is, the wind can blow at will. It is nothing to disturb him much and, if the level of water rises, great good to him.

Then, as suddenly as it came, the hurricane calmed down, luckily offshore in the Gulf of Mexico and Florida returned to its usual paradise status.

Coincidence

By pure coincidence, I am writing on the first page of this 400-page notebook on the same day as we end our five months' stay in Florida. Of course it is no big deal but it reminds me of so many other coincidences that have tinted my life.

My wife and I met while working at the same place, but we came from areas sixty miles apart. Chances are that otherwise, we may never have become acquainted. We had been married a few years when she read an ad in a newspaper about a cruise ship that could also take our motorhome with us from Canada to Europe. We got aboard the Pushkin and spent nine months touring Europe. Back to Canada working as a salesman, I attended a sales presentation given by the president of a sales agency. He hired me to join his firm where I worked seventeen years. We had never met before and could have easily gone other ways without joining forces for so long.

Many years later, as we started planning for retirement, we bought a small property in Florida. As Canadians, the fluctuation of our dollar can increase our cost in US dollars by as much as fifty percent. Over the years, these dollars rarely match but luckily they did when we bought our lot and house in 2011. Now in 2017, it would cost us 37% more and we could probably not afford it. An area where all countries rate even is when you have to be waiting in line to be served. Most times when you select the one with fewest people, you always notice another line of customers being served faster.

Odds meet in nature also. We were over sixty years old when we realised that on some days of the year, the sunset and the moonrise coincide to give an impressive show. As for rain goes unless our garden needs water, I avoid washing my car because it always rains the day after I have washed it.

In all fairness, we cannot pretend that coincidences are always for the better, but I will let others handle the sad ones. From my perspective, they need to be provoked to suddenly appear. Exposure is the common denominator in all of the above. Occurrences will happen with or without us. So all we have to do is to show-up as often as possible, in as broad a variety of happenings as we can and, this way only, unknowns stand a chance to coincide favourably.

Day On The Road

Kevin still had about twenty hours of driving when it hit him! Arthritis pain was his main nightmare any time he had to sit still for too long. So, every ninety minutes he had to stop and stretch for a while. He has had this condition for many years and learned to live with it. No, the flash he just had was not pain, it had more to do with riding in a kind of twilight zone.

Having been driving on the highway at maximum speed limit for the past five hours, he was about to call it a day. But he wondered about all he had missed on the way. Walking is the only way to enjoy plants and animals on a trail. For such a long distance, going on foot would take too much time. At the other end of the spectrum, the highway becomes like a vacuum tube sucking him to the destination. Yielding and passing kept him alert but most of the road sides were lined with trees, enhancing the tube effect.

Listening to recorded music or scanned radio channels covered most of the road noises but became repetitive after such a long journey. Trying to remember what happened along the way was just a blur. Imagining what the next few days will be like, was not much better. He kept his mind busy reading advertising billboards but few were enlightening. Licence plates of passing vehicles allowed him to play poker and to hope he would draw a perfect hand. He thought he had seen a plate with a straight flush but he had to steer quickly through the next exit before he ran out of gas.

After filling-up at the truck stop, he went into the adjacent convenience store to buy a chocolate bar, hoping it would keep him awake. Walking the store aisles, he noticed an impressive display of music discs. Next to it was a large assortment of novels on audio-discs. It had never occurred to him that he could listen to stories while driving! He was surprised to see many truckers elbow their way next to him to buy some. This is how he discovered the wonderful universe of **Morris West** and his Best Seller novel **Cassidy** while cruising through the twilight zone of his next day on the road.

Flood Zone

Every spring, rivers flood their shores as they get overwhelmed by the mountain's snow melting. Anyone living close to shore is at risk. Jane and Mike knew all that when they bought this piece of land in Rawdon. Being a thirty thousand square feet area, it is large enough to fit their new house in the middle and have enough privacy space left from neighbours' lots.

Enthusiast and skilled kayakers, this is one of their favourite rivers. It is lovely and challenging upstream and downstream from their lot during seven months of the year. Then the ice builds-up so thick on it that cross-country skiing is their other passion for most of the winter months.

Many areas along this river are recorded as possible flood zones on which you cannot get a building permit. Such is the case for the lot across from their river frontage but not for theirs. Those records go back one hundred years so they felt safe building on theirs. Records did not show how close to flooding their lot had been, just that it never did go under water. Still, being so close to danger, Mike decided to limit the risk of flooding as much as he could.

Research of the web all over the world gave him a bundle of valid input. But he got his key idea from Noah's ark. Of course he made sure to raise the ground around the house, way above the river level but also at a safe one hundred feet distance from shore. Making sure the house could float was the Noah challenge.

Based on the idea that some boats' hulls are made of concrete, he used the same formula for his basement. Rebar steel reinforced, water sealed concrete basement floor and walls had to be proportionally heavier than the house on top to make sure it would not flip over should the water raise it out of ground. Plumbing and electrical links were hooked up to unplug safely like the ones on a rocket launch.

All was well as this sixth winter on site would be over soon. They loved every minute they could be in this house. Confidence to end this 2017 winter without problems vanished when March 20 left four feet of snow on the ground. The river had already begun to thaw but the five days below freezing that followed created a giant ice jam. Heavy equipment and explosives were used to break the ice which was a mile long and up to ten feet in thickness. A week later, temperatures stayed warm for five days in a row and the spring sun sped up thaw of the river upstream but not the jam. Mike and Jane had to kayak out of their house when it became surrounded by three feet of water and still rising. Their neighbour's house across the street was on a much higher ridge and he invited them over to stay. Looking across from his living room bay window, they were all astonished to see their house across the street start floating and land six feet inland to the new river shore.

TV newscast teams rushed over to witness this floating bungalow and many videos about it turned viral on the web the same day. Engineers and architects came to study the concept that is now compulsory for any house built with a basement floor less than ten feet above the normal river water level. These floating houses are now easily identified because of their regulatory ship's type of davits holding a lifeboat on an outside side wall.

Useless Highway

I am looking ahead to the days when cars will no longer be the way to travel. It is hard to conceive this today but same could be told when horse and buggy was the only way. Change was rather slow back then and more than twenty years were needed for cars to be trusted enough to replace horses and mules. Most cars are moving along today at maximum speed and leaves much less time for the driver to enjoy the view. Your ancestor had all the time in the world while his horse often knew the way and needed much less steering than your car.

Seeking more enjoyment in roving, some people go to the other extreme. Compostelle between France and Spain is a famous way to try it. Walking along with fellow rovers, each step is felt as an accomplishment towards the goal. This trail crosses only a few roads but always on a safe path. Small Inns and restaurants cater to the trekkers building up an appetite and admiring country side vistas. Americans caught up to the idea. Their Blue Ridge Trail runs atop the Appalachians and could keep you walking in this blessed environment for many weeks.

As this phenomenon catches on more fans, technology moves along quickly. The Star-Trek molecule transponder will soon beam us up Captain! If going somewhere is your main concern, why endure unpleasant flights. Why risk being dragged off an airplane by flight attendants gone mad if you can (like it happened on United Airlines in April 2017).

This being settled, imagine that you can be at destination, the next second after you keyed in your correct username and password. What will the multitude of highways be needed for? Over the past hundred years, mankind has wasted so much farmland to build roads. As we all know, given time, nature is strong enough to grow roots through them all and eventually camouflage them under vegetation. Cars will become redundant since all will be delivered to your residence, a short while after keying your order online. Just make sure you keep your car parking space available so that your home transponder station can be conveniently located close to you.

Smart Maria

If only he had listened to her! Maria had warned Syd at least fifty times. Once again Syd got away without too much harm. But this time, his pride got seriously bruised. Set in his ways, Syd never considered changing. His work colleagues also tried to over the years but finally accepted Syd's habits. They had to admit he was not causing much inconvenience to anyone. Still, some found it strange enough to never even think of giving it a try for fear of being seen doing it.

It was when Syd worked in Port-Cartier that he was forced to act this way. The mining company he had worked for, made it a compulsory part of their emergency evacuation protocol. Anyone not complying with it would be fined and risk expulsion. The ore and various minerals they were handling could ignite and cause a fire extremely hard to extinguish. A few years ago, such an event happened so badly that half the plant burned to the ground. Every second counts; eight hundred employees evacuated safely that day but two were trapped and died on site.

The plant was far enough from the town centre that no other resident was at risk. Since employees and miners needed their cars to get to work in this remote area, ample parking was available close to the main smelting facilities. In case of emergency evacuation, each employee must run to his car and follow the evacuation route identified by security guards on site. To save precious seconds, all cars must be backed up into a parking space. This allowed forward exit reducing confusion. The two employees that died were parked the wrong way, had to wait for all others to drive by them. Being the last two cars on their way out, they were still too close and got hit by debris falling on their car when the plant exploded.

Maria knew all this but thought it was rather risky to back up the car into such a tight space as their small garage at home. Syd would not hear a thing against it. He always backed up slowly until he hit the plastic recycling bin stored in the back of the garage. Today he rushed the delicate manoeuvre because he was overdue to use the toilet. Instead of pressing the brake pedal, he hit the gas pedal, raised the back of the car over the trash bin and landed on top of his lawnmower. He almost wet himself while waiting in his car, ashamed to face smart Maria who would not miss this new chance to repeat, "I told you so".

Drink Stop

Eva and Larry live a lovely house with a good size backyard. Large trees and shrubs contour the lawn so densely that no man made structure is visible from the back of their house. Watching vegetation and wildlife evolve while eating breakfast is their favourite period of the day. So they have set a bistro style table for two with comfortable chairs in front of a large window for a good direct view on nature's daily happenings.

Each morning is different. The clouds, the sun, the rain, the flowers and other elements of the sort, get intertwined in various ways. It is as if each item managed to be the star of the show for at least one day once a year. This morning it is definitely buds day. The saying 'April showers bring May flowers' applied almost excessively this year. Lakes and rivers shores are flooded everywhere. It is still cold for the season, so the buds of the year held back a little but now, overly bloated by so much rain, they could not wait any longer. This morning is when they elected to burst. Brand new green leaves now confirm each branch's eagerness to grow. What looked like dead wood a week ago has evolved in a multitude of leaf patterns, each with its own angle on life. The Creator of such wonders is so talented that any artist would have a hard time painting it and even so, it would only be a flat copy.

Eva always liked to attract birds and small animals in her morning viewing. She had Larry build stands and brackets for bird feeders. They also installed a few bird houses in hope to have some nesting in view. But the house cat ran a sharp watch over his kingdom and limited the visitors. After fifteen years of this regime, the cat passed away and was not replaced. Squirrels now run the area but do not scare rabbits and birds that show up every day. Their swift moves are constant eye-catchers, adding motion to the picturesque sight.

Larry eventually had to remove the bird feeders because squirrels and raccoons always found a way to break into them. Bird houses did not get bird tenants but nested bees. What he replaced these with is much better. A simple plastic bowl that holds two litres of water is all it took. Laid on the ground amongst plants but in view from their table, they get a wonderful parade. Birds come to drink and bathe. Squirrels no longer chew garden hoses to drink water in them and even the rabbit stops for a drink. This water hole is so popular that they added an extra one to avoid animals having to fight for access. These are easy to maintain and inexpensive. All they have to do is change the water and clean them every two days to avoid nesting mosquitoes. What a wonderful way of getting a pleasant nature show every morning at your very own fauna Drink Stop.

Farming Brotherhood

Mindful of the role they agreed to play, all of them got on the bus. About a year ago, Fred came up with this solution. He went to all five uncles on his father's side and convinced them to join his mission for a week. A chartered bus went to pick them up at home in order to warm-up the clan spirit.

His father Ken still lived on the family farm. He had been the only of the six sons to accept farming as a lifestyle. This pristine farmland has been in their family for three generations and always produced generous crops. Fred was the only son of Ken and did not care for farming at all. So Ken ran the farm alone since his wife Mary passed away two years ago. His hired staff of three was close to retirement age and hiring was difficult. This is why Fred convinced all to come to help his father sell the farm.

The six-bedroom farmhouse became like the clan fortress when the bus unloaded a total of ten relatives. The plan was to get everyone busy with a specific task. Four days later, their operation ran smoothly enough to invite buyers. Sure enough, a lot of prospect buyers showed up, from as far as China and Austria to visit. Offers were very interesting but surprisingly, all were refused. This reborn clan liked their joint venture so much that they now have been at it for five years and family members have all moved to the rightfully renamed Brotherhood Farm.

Water-Grid

Climate change spurs extreme weather occurrences more frequently. Winter days will often swing from heavy snow to freezing rain. Deep freeze temperatures will then stay for weeks rending sidewalks and streets dangerous and very difficult to clear. People will hope to see spring show-up early. Freezing in April is rare in Montreal, Quebec but still happens often enough that new planting is safer only after mid-May. Everyone's hope is high this year of

2017 to get a more generous flower bloom from the almost constant downpour since the arrival of spring.

What changed is that it did not stop raining in May 2017. Rivers started flooding shores that had never been flooded for more than one hundred years. The Mississippi and a lot of other rivers did the same in America. Authorities and insurance companies were spending millions while citizens were deeply depressed, unable to salvage their drowned belongings. Troops were asked for help with military equipment building temporary dams and bridges.

Meanwhile, other areas were affected by unusual drought. Garden states like Florida and California were so short of rain that the crops dried in the field. This attracted grasshopper invasions and generated a few sand storms. The morning fog reeked because it was loaded with smoke from bush fires hardly contained. Visibility was so bad; highways often had to be closed and dangerously limited evacuation routes.

A solution was introduced by Hydro-Quebec teamed up with Trans-Canada Pipeline. Their joint venture was named the Water-Grid. Being an important electric power generating utility producing mainly hydroelectricity, Hydro-Quebec already managed a lot of dams. Regulating river levels, to fill reservoirs feeding turbines while allowing enough water flow for navigation downstream, was their daily challenge. But when the dams are all full from spring thaw and steady rain for weeks, downstream areas are flooded. This is where Trans-Canada Pipeline was invited to help. By laying a network of huge underground water pipes, water could be dispatched to drought areas all over America and Canada. Using the corridors under electric power lines, pipes and pumping stations were used all over the continent as a grid. Only water can be run through these, eliminating the risk of fire or the spilling of polluting fluids. Firefighters could now depend on this nearer supply of water to extinguish forest wildfires like the ones that burned during a month and devastated a gigantic area of Northern Alberta.

This ample supply of fresh water (not sea water) was sold just like electricity by all utilities already linked. Only excess water could be sold; independent surveillance made sure that lakes and rivers could not be excessively drained. Funded partly by governments but mostly by insurance companies, it saved a fortune in avoiding future fire and flood related damages to properties and infrastructure all thanks to the North American Water Grid.

Barayo Potluck

Most towns in the world have soon after their creation, built a church or temple of some kind. In the centre of the village, the church steeple would be the pride of residents for many generations. A charismatic priest or preacher made a big difference in attracting parishioners and getting their support.

Barayo, our little town of three thousand souls today, was originally mostly consisting of a few farmers spread along the shores of Lake St-Louis. A Sulpician priest named Barayo managed to group their efforts and build the first chapel. The Town kept his name but did not keep the building. Over time, wealthy families from Montreal built summer cottages in Barayo taking advantage of its fresh air and sailing on the lake.

Immigrants from as far as China and Germany have now populated our small town into a broad diversity. Many have remained attached to religious practice and travel for as much as an hour to visit a church, temple or synagogue of their liking. Their weekly gathering prompts civilities, helped by words of wisdom from a presiding minister. They also enjoy meeting people of good faith, sharing their striving for a better world.

Short of such a gathering event, Barayo citizens met briefly at the monthly Town Council meeting, at the swimming pool, the Curling Club or at many other community activities. But most of these encounters were brief and left little time for mingling. Getting to know each other is paramount for a healthy and safe society.

So, the 'Barayo Potluck' was created by the Citizens' Association. Strategically set for dinner on the fourth Thursday of every month, it also assured a good meal to low income residents. Medication or other major expenses made them struggle until the first of next month to receive a pension check allowing to go buy groceries. Proud cooks came to the Potluck carrying their favourite meal and turned the event into an impressive feast. The Farm house community centre was busy at 4:30 with volunteers setting up tables and chairs. By 5pm new comers were welcomed and chatting was in full swing. At 5:30 everyone had chosen a seat, set their own tableware and drinks and, using their own plate served themselves from the generous buffet. An invited guest was given fifteen minutes to address the community at 6:30. At 7pm the room clean-up started as people resumed conversations and set dates for other neighbourly rendezvous. Other communities are now copying the event after some came as guests and witnessed the camaraderie and fondness of attendees to the now famous Barayo Potluck.

Dandelion

Chances are that we have now merged into the warmer part of the year. It is not unusual in mid-May to still get a few nights below freezing. But for the most part, no deep freeze should affect us for the next five months. It is not an absolute certainty but rather an expected perennial occurrence for the Montreal, Quebec area of Canada.

Knowing that we are at risk of losing new plants to freezing, we wait impatiently. On May 16th this year, we could not delay this pleasure any longer. Early this Tuesday morning, we soared through the wonders of our local nursery. So many colours, textures and fragrances shake off the grey layer still coating our winterized soul.

For the south and sunniest side of our house, we chose a few buckets of gazanias. Their blossom last all summer but close shop every night. So each morning features a reopening of dozens of beautiful and bright yellow, orange, pink and red flowers on a dark green foliage background. The west side of our backyard is lined by six huge trees. In the middle part, under two large maple trees, we are having a hard time growing anything substantial. Anywhere close to the trunks, even ferns are barely allowed to survive. The maple roots suck all the energy they need to support their sixty feet high leafed umbrella. This is the prominent view from our breakfast table. We will not leave it to simple grass or weeds. So this year we planted eighteen 'Ajuga Reptans Mahogany'. Their broad burgundy and glossy leaves edge well and contrast with the lawn. Over the next month they will spread all over this open space and create a strikingly waving carpet. Tulips, hyacinths and other bulbs now burst straight out of our house's façade garden. Unfortunately their flowers last only a few weeks, so we planted a dozen pots of 'New Guinea Harmony'. The variety we found are of a bright pink with red patches. Their shiny broad green leaves boost their beauty and enlighten the shrubs sharing this prime location. Five new 'Japanese Ferns Branford Beauty' amongst these flowers at the base of our ten year old 'Ginkgo Biloba on stem' give our house an uplifted curb appeal.

Most plants are now following the lead and allow each day, hundreds of buds and flowers to join the show. Thinking back at how it all started, we must admit that one flower was the leader. Its bright yellow blossom is now covering most landscapes. Force is to admit that the dominant season opener is definitely the dandelion. Rarely has it been surprised by snow or frost so, when it spreads in full bloom, we can rest assured that it is safe to go all out on flower power.

Dozen

Way back, when none of us had any electronic gadgets to help us add and subtract, what did people do? Most of us today will not even make the effort to multiply or divide and will simply reach for the nearby smart phone or computer to do it. Even before they existed, portable calculators were always in close reach to save us time. In so doing, we are gradually losing this ability to calculate, if we ever had it!

Slide rules were the hi-tech state of the art for a while. Some of them were quite elaborate and you needed a lot of training to master them. They also required excellent vision to properly read all those fine lines. Many rockets must have missed their targets since only a one degree error at source becomes miles apart in space.

A good memory was essential. Mathematical tables were printed on the back of most students' notebooks for easy reference. So everybody knew by heart that nine times seven was sixty-three and fifty-four divided by nine was six. At age ten if not before, all children could add, subtract, multiply and divide any mix of digits from one to ten with an instantaneous response only on brain power, not batteries.

The Chinese still use their fail safe abacus that has been in use for thousands of years. Surely other civilizations have developed their own way to count. But I found out recently that one universal way was in service before any other apparatus. One human hand was all that was needed. Counting on fingers, unless you have lost a few, explains how over two hands, many items have been grouped in multiples of ten. But how did the dozen originate? Without making an extensive list, we all know that eggs, inches, beer, oysters and many other things are strangely traded in dozens, not tens. Apparently, the human hand is the dozen's source. And only one hand is needed so the other can carry whatever. Using your thumb, you must touch two knuckles and the tip of each of your four fingers. This adds up to twelve and could be used without any language barrier in trading near the Tower of Babel, over two thousand years ago.

Mall Trekking

All they wanted was a way to stay in shape. Doing it together was challenging. Pauline retired a few months ago, but Bob stopped his career ten years ago. He got most of his exercise from working on their house maintenance. Like his generation of men, work filled most of his life so, the little free time left was for resting in his favorite reclining Lazy-Boy armchair. Pauline stayed in better shape from working mostly standing behind a beauty products counter in a department store where she worked most of the day.

She also always liked dancing and never missed her weekly class.

Walking became their preferred shape-up shared activity. A large park was only a few blocks away. Getting there through different streets and going on various trails provided some interesting changes. Occasionally they would drive to a mountain in the area. Three of these with public trails are less than an hour away and the closest only at a fifteen minutes' drive. All offered hours of trekking into safe wilderness and fresh air. Weather often changed their plans, so they found a new, air-conditioned way to stay on the move.

Bob never enjoyed shopping. Still, a few times a year, Pauline almost had to drag him to the mall. Their last visit was because she could not stand to see his old raincoat so he had to come with her to buy a replacement and shop for a new refrigerator at the same time. This week, it was the dishwasher failure that got them there together. The four stores that sold major appliances are located at each of the opposing ends of the mall. After visiting them all, they stopped for lunch at the food court to discuss and select a model. They agreed on one they both liked and also agreed to come back to walk. Looking around them, they could not help noticing that the majority of shoppers were retirees like them. Who else can be here midweek during the day while most people are working or at school? Some looked like experienced mall trekkers. Even in winter, they wore comfortable stretchy clothes and good lightweight walking shoes.

A locker at the mall entrance is where they stored their warm overcoats and boots. Many stores now opened a branch in the mall to attract this new clientele.

So, next time you visit your local mall, pay attention to the crowd, if any. Sure enough you will notice a lot of active old folks. And keep your head up and peripheral view alert because they walk fast. Just stay out of their way in case they cannot side-step fast enough to avoid you in their energetic Mall Trekking session.

Sainte-Sabine

Nancy and Andrew live in a comfortable apartment in the city. Conveniently located close to relatives and shops, it meets all their expectations as a main residence. But since both of them were raised in the country, they needed an occasional retreat away from congested downtown. Sainte-Sabine is where they elected to set up camp.

The Caravelle Campground is surrounded by farmland and is very peaceful. It is such a secure haven for kids and families that many residents live there for the warmest six months of the year. Nancy and Andrew feel very lucky to have a choice site. One of the few without a neighbour across the street, they have an open view on the public pool. Their forty-foot trailer offers all comforts of their winter home but also has an exquisite terrace. Only one step down from the trailer and a step up above ground, it is a perfect setting for leisurely hours. An extended area at the same level is screened to protect the dining table for six. From this vantage patio, they are immersed in bird songs, kids' laughs and wind activated leaves' ballet. Nancy is my wife's sister. We make it a point to visit them in Sainte-Sabine at least once a year. This last Sunday of May offered perfect weather. Wanting to be there at eleven, we took the highway and got there in ninety minutes. Road construction detours are always an unknown and a source of worry. But this ride was without delay. It was warm enough to eat outside. The beef and chicken brochettes were barbecued just right by Andrew's expert touch. They were great hosts and fun company for conversation on a broad array of topics. Time flies fast and by mid-afternoon, we had to leave in order to avoid heavy end of weekend traffic.

Instead of going back the same way, Google Map helped me identify backcountry roads. That was such an interesting road trip. Our first surprise was Venise-en-Québec. Its quaint Côte d'Azur feeling along the wonderful Baie-Missisquoi was buzzing with a happy crowd. Then the Noyan Bridge over the Richelieu River gave us an impressive view over the beautiful area. As we came closer to Hemmingford, farmland was all over. Gigantic machinery had manicured the land to a smooth black earth surface. For the next thirty minutes we were in awe looking at what is probably the best vegetable growing land in Québec. It is comforting to know that such gardening remains all around the island of Montreal ready to feed millions of people. And city slickers can even live in the garden area for a while like they do so well in Sainte-Sabine.

Home Mall

On-line shopping has now grown to a point where its sales are higher than through conventional retail stores. This is obvious when you visit most shopping malls across Canada. A good example is the Faubourg de l'Ile Shopping Centre in Pincourt, Québec.

Out of the eighty retail store spaces in the mall, only twenty-two now barely survive. A few large retailers are still attracting some consumers. But if Walmart, Canadian Tire or Pharmaprix were to close shop, the whole mall would die. Pincourt is still a lovely town to live in. Mostly consisting of single dwelling detached houses, it also has apartments and condominiums near the mall. But across the bridge in

Vaudreuil, a whole new shopping area was built. People favoured its broader offering to the detriment of their thirty-year-old mall.

A visionary group found an interesting way to revive this mall and many others. Most malls are located in prime areas well surrounded with easy access roads, infrastructure and residential neighbourhoods. But you need a car or public transport to get there. For retirees and older generations still in good enough shape, walking to the stores would be the preferred choice. So, this Excellence Residence Group acquired at a good price, such slow business malls to repurpose them.

Adding an underground parking and two to six floors of apartments above the mall gave them a whole new twist. Whatever the weather, even in a nasty winter snowstorm, happy old folks can now ride the elevator down to the mall level and buy all necessities without ever needing warmer clothing. Families and friends come to visit them more often while on their way to their own shopping on site. The rooftop was turned into gardens with many easy chairs and swings. A few shaded areas protected from the wind offered striking vistas on the lake, just a few blocks away from their livelier Home Mall.

Upgrade

Update or Upgrade, that is the question! Of course, 'To Be or Not To Be' remains important. But while you feel that your being is presently on a safe ride, you must risk a decision and reply before you are allowed reaching the next step. Almost every day, a smart phone or computer will prompt you with questioning screen information.

A lot of these processes can be set in advance and done automatically. But then, while you are in the middle of some operation or transaction, it will jam your device or slow it down to execute its routine. On a few occasions, I thought my phone had died. Its screen turned totally black and would not show any sign of life. Before its brain could be permanently affected, I pressed each button in various sequences in hope for resuscitation but it was to no avail. Mysteriously, after a rest of a few hours, it worked perfectly again but showed no sign of remorse for having upset me. It was probably updating its operating system and never considered it important to inform me.

My computer is set to manage such operations with a notice when it is due and asks me to do it now or later. These notices will pop up on my screen too often, taking advantage of my captive attention to offer additional features. They will even change the display format from the last time forcing me to read it all before I click. My credit card number is what they are after. Now that they hold me as a serious prospective buyer, they persist on offering me new options. They presume that I bought the Premium version of their software to meet my requirements back then. Six months later, they hope I will be interested by unique features only offered by the Supreme version. And this Upgrade will cost me 59,99$ or only 6$ per month for a year.

A friendlier way would be to receive an email from each software company, only when a new service or upgrade is available. An occasional newsletter could report on tricks of the trade shared by users. Customer service staff should be replying to chats from users with application issues. Taking good care of your devices will let them operate for over ten years, but don't bank on it. Someone somewhere wants you to buy a new one. And forget about repair shops because replacement parts are not sold. The way they will get you to upgrade against your will is by obsoleting the operating system or changing coaxial cables to fibre optics and going from analog to digital. Meanwhile back at the dump, the pile gets bigger.

In a few more decades, the mountain of obsolete junk will be so gigantic, they will convert them into ski resorts claiming, "Join us Up Grade".

Seeding Change

The weather had been great all day. Even now after seven in the evening, it was still 21°C and I felt like sitting on the patio for a while. Resting was all I had in mind, perhaps reading a novel. But some strange force pulled me otherwise. We had to mail a cheque to our accountant so, I put on my sneakers and walked to the Canada Post mail box.

Located just a street block away from our house it was not too strenuous after my long work day. At about ten this morning, when the sun had sucked up most of the morning dew, my powered-wheels mower pulled me for a walk. Even if it is self-propelled, it is challenging to keep up with it. Emptying its heavy bag in the recycling bin every five minutes increases the walking distance. This run should also reap the thousands of fallen maple samaras and, good riddance for that.

By noon both the mower and I were put to rest. Considering it as a good workout, I would not trade it for time inside a fitness centre. But I was glad it was done and I enjoyed resting my legs while sitting for lunch. The afternoon work was much harder. Grass was refusing to grow in some areas of our lawn. Previous seeding covered by good planting earth did not work and, dandelions were spreading all over. On my knees for two hours, I cleared weeds and debris from these areas. Then using the 'Supreme' brand of seeds that grew well on one of my neighbour's lawn, I covered it with enriched earth recommended by the same brand. Raking-it all-in was then just in time before the heavy rain on the forecast for tomorrow.

I was aching all over and very dirty when I finally got in the shower. Tortellini-Sauce-Rosée hit the spot perfectly for dinner. That is what probably gave me a new boost to walk to the mail box. Walking in front of the house of our backyard neighbour, I noticed people sitting on the front steps, smoking. When I came back from the mail box at the street corner, they were still there. I stopped to ask them about Rena that I had not seen lately. We usually had a few chats every summer along our mutual backyard fence. But not this spring and her son had told us she was not well. This young couple sitting on the steps was her other son and his wife. He said she passed away five days ago from a heart attack. I said I was coming to say hello to Rena. Her sudden death really affected me and I offered them my condolences and help if needed. Chances are that Rena's sons will sell the house in the near future. Hopefully the new neighbours will be as friendly as this day's simple plan for seeding change.

Golden Age Space

Couples work hard all their lives, starting from a small love nest apartment costing them a large part of their joint income. In need of all basic furniture and appliances, his parents' old couch and her mother's old stove will do just fine. A local second-hand furniture store is where they can afford to shop for all except their bed and mattress that she insists on buying new. Their first child fills them with joy and brings luck in their individual careers. In need of more space, a first mortgage is approved and they move into a row house populated mostly by young families.

This small house becomes their stepping stone to real estate. Ten years later, its value has increased enough to help them buy a bungalow in Beaconsfield. Now with two children, they need four bedrooms. One room will be used as their home office to support these two professionals who on some days could work from home. The large basement family room and adjacent home cinema assure years of enjoyment.

Thirty years later, their children have left to start their own ventures. Now in their sixties, the parents love having their grandchildren over and they host many family gatherings all year. But their children have their own social life and BBQ parties where they live most weekends. The Beaconsfield bungalow is now too large for our old folks. They renovated it a few times over the years but soon, major expenditures will be needed. The septic tank, leach field, the roof, the driveway, the windows and the heat pump are all approaching the end of their expected life.

While they mourned the loss of too many friends that did not make it to sixty years of age and many others affected by serious illness, they decide to retire at sixty-five. The bungalow is requiring too much maintenance and worry so they sell it. Apartments in Beaconsfield are mostly in the area next to the noisy highway and railway. So they move to Beaurepaire where they rent a lovely two-bedroom apartment in a quiet area. Their new love nest is within walking distance to the village convenience stores and tennis club. This is where they meet dozens of happy retirees and new friends making the most of the Golden Age.

Past Post

Way back then, most communities would be formed by settlers coming to work at a factory. Its growing business required more staff trained on site with new skills. These were permanent enough jobs that a new neighborhood was built close to the plant. A general store would soon open to supply people's needs. Some leaders formed a village council that would eventually set a plan and have streets built in an orderly way. Next to the general store, little shops would open and the area would be soon designated as Main Street. At least one church would be funded and built by parishioners dedicated to their faith and being comforted by frequent gatherings. Not long after, the barber shop and the Post Office would spring up out of the ground.

Writing to relatives was often the main way to communicate. Plant employees were at work for long hours six days a week. Only rich people had a telephone, so the telegraph was the affordable way to deliver an urgent message abroad. Travelling to visit family and friends was only a last resort. Everyone anxiously awaited the mail man's passage and hoped he was bringing good news. The Post Office was always a busy place with everyone eager to forward the latest news to loved ones. The Post Master knew everybody. Nosy fellows would loiter by his counter hoping to hear about the latest happenings that could beef up conversations at home later that day. The population's quilt was so tightly knit-bound together that it was hard to keep a secret for very long.

Codes are what changed it all. Postal codes helped mail sorting. Automated mail processing plants handled the bulk of envelopes. Parcels started being bar coded and processed just as fast. Only minimal sorting was left to be done by local Post Offices so most of them were closed. The one in Dorset was a fairly large three-storey building, each floor with two-thousand square feet of space. Still located on Main Street, next to the barber shop, it surprisingly stood empty during four years. Too large for most retail shops but too small for most businesses, it was a perfect fit for FurnHotel. Laura started this business only twelve years ago, but she has worked in the hotel furnitures market for the past thirty years. The staff of twenty-five at FurnHotel marvels about their new office windows with a view on the lake. It is just a short walk away from restaurants and shops on Main Street and, the small Post Office counter, just across the street, inside the Drug Store.

Bedford by the Lake

The population in Bedford has been steady at about three thousand for the past ten years. Located at a short thirty minutes' drive from the downtown area of a metropolis, it has surprisingly preserved a feel of the country side and fresh air. It was in 1686 that the first houses were built in Bedford. These settlers were followed by generations of hard-working farmers uprooting stumps and moving boulders for years. The dense forests slowly made space for crops and grazing cattle.

When the railroad was built across the country, downtowners started travelling. Wanting to get away from the smoke and noisy turmoil of the city, some built a cottage in Bedford. Its three miles of shores on the lake were soon fringed with summer camps.

Within about a hundred years, most of them were replaced by larger houses fully equipped to live in all year round. Inland side streets were built to allow the increasing flow of new residents. In 1930, a train station was built and offered daily service to commuters on their way to work downtown.

Since 1921, Bedford has had a mayor and town council setting the rules of the land development. Making sure the future would maintain its uniqueness of large lots, by-laws stated that the minimum size lot would be 15,000 square feet. This also complied with sanitatization control of septic tanks and leach fields. Zoning was established to protect the single dwelling status for most of the town territory. Other areas were set for commercial and industrial usage.

When the last farmer passed away, the town council acquired his prime piece of land located in the middle of town. Most of it was on the lakefront and included 1,200 feet of shore. The huge farmhouse was converted into a community centre and the vast land into parks. As the town grew and tax income allowed forecasting surpluses, zoning made provision for more community facilities. Over the years, the town built a library, a swimming pool, an indoor curling rink and six tennis courts. A seniors' residence was also planned in the area but was only allowed next to the commercial zone and railroad. Residents were aware that their town had more of green spaces than most towns in Canada but were still against building apartments for seniors on the former farmland. The town council considered it political suicide to support such a project.

Growing vegetables in a greenhouse on the residence's roof is what made it happen. The new apartments building for seniors would be located on the same lot as the popular community garden. Numerous volunteer citizens who wanted to live there outnumbered the recalcitrant who finally admitted they looked forward to being able to visit or even live into this Eden. Combined with the building's atrium, the greenhouse roof will maintain its brightly lit green space appeal all year round, even during the cold, icy and otherwise sombre winter months.

Farming on the Roof

As towns spread their tentacles, it is sad to see rich farmland turning into paved streets and shopping malls. Luckily ZUFA brings farming back in the same area. ZUFA founders were students in biochemistry and computer science. Using proven hydroponic farming methods, they mastered them to obtain optimum crops.

The process is relatively light weight since plants grow in a small amount of peat moss, much lighter than regular farming soil. Sunlight is paramount and a greenhouse is the best way to get it while controlling the environment. Not using soil, they did not need ground space, now so scarce close to populated areas. So ZUFA looked for available roof space.

A few blocks from their small downtown apartment in Montreal, Quebec, ZUFA founders spotted the perfect roof. The six-storey building was built in 1920 by an important clothing manufacturer. This company still uses most of it, but they have vacated the two lower floors. New tenants on these floors are mostly sweatshops in the fashion industry. A total of a thousand employees work in this building and most of them live in the neighborhood.

At first the building owner was reluctant to even consider someone messing with the flat roof and possibly causing damages while going bankrupt. But the 50,000-square-foot farming roof was so appealing that ZUFA Farms formulated assurance and guarantees to offset all objections raised by the building owner. The concept had already been tested with success in at least ten other cities in the world. The greenhouse structure met the local building code, and the roof modifications were possible without disturbing businesses in operation below. A huge crane delivered the structure on the roof and a specialized contractor assembled it in a week. The ZUFA team preparedness was so spectacular that the first seed was planted only one month later. Sophisticated software monitored temperature, humidity and light allowing production day and night, all year round. Another month later, workers in the building were invited to ZUFA Farms' first open house. Visitors were astonished in view of so many perfect tomatoes, eggplants, lettuce, etc. that the whole production was sold that same day. Most signed up as members to reserve their vegetables every week.

Grocers kept a close watch and the following year, a food store invited ZUFA to set up a farm on its roof. As a normal grocery sourcing point for residents they all subscribed to ZUFA to reserve a vegetable basket stored for them in a specific area of the store. Other customers could also enjoy the fresh produce picked from the plant the same day and nicely displayed on the grocery shelves for hand picking as needed. Packaging and transportation expenses being avoided, prices remained the same but freshness, taste, scent and texture could not be better.

Traditional in-ground farming remained important and essential for heavier and bulkier crops like pumpkins and corn. The construction code is now being changed so that any new building can accommodate Farming on the Roof to save the land and feed more people.

Workless Mind

You work all your life and if you are lucky, you earn a decent and honest living. Retirement with some savings and a good enough pension is a vague concept when you are in your twenties. Relatives and advertising repeat so often its importance that you save a little every year, slowly filling your retirement bucket. Some get to it sooner than others. In my case, I was forty when I started taking this seriously.

Every week, work colleagues and acquaintances would want to discuss the matter with me. Trading ideas is a big part of the retirement planning game. Some thrive on tracking the stock market every day to buy low and sell high. I could not see myself enslaved by this pattern considering that more than half of the people doing it have lost a lot at it. This rat race has no bottom and what is low, is never at the lowest and hard work savings can vanish when shares turn worthless.

Again with a strong dose of luck, you get to work in a field that you enjoy and that yields reasonably good earnings. Having been at it for thirty years and more, you have attained some respect and you get to play a rewarding role. As you get closer to your sixties, you notice a change. Ways of the younger generations are different and as they activate their own network, it becomes harder for you to stay linked to the leading trends. Your own energy is starting to show signs of much slower cycles to fully recharge.

Then it hits you! Some of your friends go on retirement and urge you to join them. Still minded to keep your eyes on the ball of your daily game, you claim that you have too much fun at work to stop now. But then you hear of so many people your age getting sick or dying in their sixties that you too, throw in the towel.

Going from being busy working to nothing is quite a culture shock. Danger awaits people who get depressed after a few months of inactivity. What saved me is that I started writing. Now free to read about any topics of my choosing, I discovered the privilege of having the time to form my own opinion. Often I would even conceive a solution to a problem menacing the community. In hope of helping I write to decision makers of corporations and political leaders of all levels. Municipal, provincial and federal officials get my input and I get the comforting feeling that I did my share. The positive side effect is my mind stays sharp on a broader more interesting spectrum of matters than most jobs I have had. Definitely, I hope that my future as a retiree will always allow me to afford, to never be feeling deprived from being workless.

Life Detector

Freedom of will is so valuable, yet some people fight for it all their life and never get it. Others take it to the other extreme and want to be left alone so much that they are found dead in their home two weeks after having a heart attack alone and free!

When this happens to someone living in a single dwelling house, it may take even longer to be noticed. A bad omen for the future occupants, it has a lesser effect on neighbours. But it is not so when it happens in an apartment building. Trusting the people across the hall or next door on the same floor is beyond hope for refugees having survived a hellish part of their life. Ultimately, authorities around the world implemented a new failsafe lifesaving concept.

Based on the smoke detector acceptance, a Life Detector was developed. Using the now reliable motion detector technology, this one turns on a night light in the bathroom and looks like all standard ones but will detect only humans, not pets. Next to it on the bathroom wall, there would be at least one regular light switch that is manually operated. It would save you from having to wave at the switch to keep the room lit while you sit on the toilet or relax in your bath. The discrete light sensor is wired to a small red light emitting diode located on the wall in the corridor outside your apartment. An integrated circuit will turn on the red light if no movement was detected for more than a day. An On and an Off button on the sensor switch will also let you operate them manually. If these buttons are pressed together for two seconds, the Life Detector will be triggered to off position when you leave your property for a prolonged period. The next time the motion sensor will detect movement, it will be reset to detect inactivity.

People living on your floor can now act sooner and perhaps save your life. Seeing your red signal, they would knock on your door or phone you. If no one answers, the building superintendent will be asked to open your door and check if anything is wrong. A few apartment complexes have tested the life detector for a year, and a person was saved in every case. One instance was so dramatic that firefighters were called to break down the front door that had an extra lock. The tenant was on the floor unconscious but was brought back to life in-extremis. Keeping a sense of privacy is the challenge but the Life Detector is quickly becoming a basic requirement in worldwide building codes.

Right Here and Now

What a lovely day it was. For once in a long time, Jim had not paid attention to the weather forecast. So when he felt how warm it was, he made the effort to eat breakfast outside. By the time he wiped the patio table clean and set the stored cushions on the chairs, it was 7:30am. The sun was strong but still low, so part of the patio was in the area shaded by the house.

This was a perfect morning with only a few patches of white puffy clouds slowly drifting along. The gazanias, triggered by this new daylight boost, started opening up to spread colourful petals. Probably roused by the same phenomena, this was the moment Sonia woke up, opened the night shades over her bedroom window, and could not help smiling. Just a glance was all she needed to think of how blessed they were to bask in such a peaceful setting.

Like most mornings, a curious rabbit stopped by to stare at them. Dandelions are its favourite treats, and it finds lots of them here. Knowing that no house cat is in residence, the rabbit feels safe with Sonia and Jim. They are impressed to see how skillfully it cuts the stem at the base and as it sucks it in like spaghetti, the rabbit saves the yellow dandelion bud as the last and tastiest gulp. To attract birds, a few bird baths are strategically positioned to be in view from where they sit. A bluebird is the first to show up for its morning splash. Many others spot it and take turns to freshen up for a new day.

As early as seven in the morning, lawnmowers can ruin a truly contemplative breakfast, but not today. The cicada is the one who breaks the silence to proudly announce the imminence of a warm day. Making sure everyone gets the message, it repeats it at regular intervals until a crow spots the cicada. Its silence is replaced by the crow's call of the predator who yells its dismay when it misses a pray. Cardinals join this opera, listening to the message before responding with a proper repartee. Having nothing on the agenda for the day, Sonia and Jim decide to take advantage of this perfect weather for window washing while being privileged spectators to serene wildlife performers Right Here and Now.

Clearview

The temperate climate of Montreal, Quebec is so changing that we have to take each day at face value and make the most of it to be happy. Bad weather days can be challenging but weather forecast give us a chance to see them coming. Unless you have a set appointment that you would rather not change, you keep your head down and bull your way through the day.

An unexpected phone call can change programmed activities set a long time in advance. A sick relative asking for your help will send you rushing across town. But you cannot sit by the phone most of the time unless, of course, you work at a 911 emergency office. So, you are facing your own to-do list in hope of meeting the expectations of your loved ones as well as your own. Interestingly enough, pleasant activities are just another bullet on the list but are rarely pushed down the list as chores can be. Sometimes a reminder signal must be sent to your brain to put it all in perspective.

Everything being better in due time, we often learn the hard way that the put-off chore eventually becomes a major breakdown causing an accident or flooding your basement. Living in your own house is quite a privilege and is linked to a lot of responsibilities. The season dictates how to prioritize the to-do list. In the spring, we are anxious to see new leaves appear. Soon after, trees are in full bloom and marvel us with fragrances that we have missed for over six months. June introduces new seeds and falls withered flowers from trees. Such debris cumulate so much that it uses most of the day to clean them away. Window washing is overdue but would be useless now that maple samaras fall by the thousands. Mosquitoes and flies are so omnipresent in early July that we cannot open windows wide to clean them and risk an invasion. Then it happens; July 20th shows up and is perfect. Avoiding being burned by the sun, we start on the shady side of the house. As soon as another side is shaded, we vacuum the screen, remove all the spiders' nests and bug stains. Soon the windows are squeaky clean, this burden chore done perfectly and almost in a fun way because, it was done in due time and rewarded by a Clear View on tomorrow.

Urge for Food

Grocery shopping is a weekly chore that I enjoy turning into a pleasant event. Conscious that we are so privileged to live in a blessed part of the world where there are groceries at a short distance with shelves full of a generous assortment of healthy foods to choose from. Our food budget is busted every year due to the constantly rising prices. So we struggle to make ends meet and survive.

The mystery tour of the aisles starts at the store door. This is where you get to have a first look at the people booked on the same cruise as you. Unless you have set it up, it is only fortuity that has brought your group on board at this same time and place. I rarely meet someone I know, still I try to smile and be courteous to these strangers. Most time they reflect my behavior and render pleasant our numerous cross aisle encounters.

But timing is everything. A few years ago, our food replenishment was done as quickly as possible, whenever we found time. Driving back from work, stuck in traffic for an hour, a grocery venture felt like a pit stop. Hungry and angry was how most people looked like at 6pm in and around that store. Once you were done fighting to get the best parking spot, you were lucky if your store had a separate entrance door because it would have been dangerous trying to go in through the exit door while people rushed out of it, ramming a loaded cart towards you. Still minded to slalom your way through road traffic, you skillfully avoid stalled carts and proudly emerge at the other end of most aisles.

Sure enough it happens every time and often in the noodles aisle. Two old friends meet in the middle of it and start chatting as if they were alone on the planet. People like you are coming in from both ends. You are so focused on finding your favorite spaghetti sauce that it is only when you found it that you notice how jammed you are, right in the middle of this long aisle. You analyse movement and go the most flowing way. You finish ticking off your list with the ice cream and other frozen foods hoping you will not be delayed and have them thaw.

Selecting which cash register with fewer people before you line up, you start emptying your cart on the conveyor. It should go fast since the persons in front of you have small loads. But they present discount coupons and one is not valid. They insist so the cashier calls for help from the manager who of course is busy. You notice the people at the other cashier moving out while you debate if you should reload your cart and change rows but too late. People are already lining up behind you and at every other rows.

Retirement means we can now avoid such nightmare outings. Staying alert and street wise is our challenge to make sure our timing is right when we feel the urge for food.

Crossroad Encounter

Yesterday was a beautiful sunny day but it was almost the last day in the life of Mary and her ten-year-old son Andrew. She was driving the family Chevy SUV going south on Churchill Street on her way to the Sailing Club. Andrew was sitting on the back seat very focused on a game he was playing on his mother's smart tablet. He was hoping he could win the game before they reached destination, only half a kilometre away. They were going sailing with Peter and the tablet was not allowed on board.

Sandra was on a tight schedule. The closing procedure at the notary had taken more time than usual. She hated being late for an appointment, particularly with a new customer. As a successful real-estate agent she was popular in the West Island area that she knew very well. Reading the street addresses, she was only a few houses away now. Driving west on Westchester, she stopped her luxurious Porsche SUV at the corner of Churchill. This gave her time to look again at the address on her phone.

Both Mary and Sandra had driven through this neighborhood numerous times but had never met. Their first encounter was brutal and almost fatal for Mary and her son. Having been stopped for about half a minute, Sandra noticed Mary's SUV driving towards her but figured she would have to make a stop at the corner of Westchester. Sandra stepped on the gas pedal and rammed the side of Mary's SUV who never had time to avoid her. Mary had the right of way and was stunned by the impact that happened so fast. Both she and her son were sprayed with broken glass but luckily without any major injury, only a few cuts bleeding a little. The two SUVs were so damaged that both had to be towed away. Sandra was not hurt except for her pride. An ambulance took Mary and Andrew to the hospital to treat their wounds and recuperate from their shock. Neighbours who had heard the impact boom and commotion gathered and offered help. Firemen and police arrived quickly and the ambulance soon after. The common opinion is that this crossroad should have a regulatory stop sign for all four directions, not only two. They issued and signed a joint letter to the Mayor and Town Council to have it done before a fatal encounter can occur.

All Cows Eat Grass

Every Good Boy Does Fine! This mnemonic phrase has helped improve my piano playing tremendously. As most French-speaking Quebecois I have learned some music theory at school. Notes are designated by Do Ré Mi Fa Sol La Si and it is always hard to remember where one belonged on a line or an interval of a staff. Once you have figured it out for the key of Sol used by your right hand on the piano, you have to memorize how the left hand often plays the notes using the different key of Fa.

Piano playing is challenging but also a great pleasure. I started by taking lessons when I was fifty. My weekly lesson was helping me play songs I liked. My teacher was patient enough that I eventually was able to play fifteen tunes and even sing along with a few of them. When I retired from full-time work eight years later, I stopped taking piano lessons and figured I could manage on my own, now that I had more free time to practise. I learned a few more tunes but still had trouble matching the note on paper with the one on the piano keyboard. After a lot of repetition I noticed that muscle memory was allowing me to play more fluently. But, skipping a few notes or playing them with the wrong finger also became repetitive since I was no longer reading the notes I was playing. Then it became obvious that even learning new songs this way was arduous and erratic.

Determined to get better at it, I followed my friend Ralph's advice and called a local piano teacher. Joann is a reputed concert pianist and piano teacher that lives only a few houses away from ours. Being able to walk over to my lessons convinced me that she was the one who could best help me. But she was not so sure. Being American, she did not teach in the Do Ré Mi way. She probably sensed how determined I was to learn the English way and we both agreed to give it a try. In the first lesson she was surprised that I did not know about the mnemonic "Every Good Boy Does Fine" and "F A C E" to remember the lines and intervals for the right hand. "Good Boys Do Fine Always" is the other mnemonic along with "All Cows Eat Grass" to remember the notes on each line and interval played by the left hand on the piano. These tricks of the piano trade help me speed up music notes reading.

Paying attention to the value of each note is my other challenge in order to stay in tempo. It is a long and treacherous road for a sixty year old man but every week, with my teachers' help, I get a little better at it. And I look forward to being able to play with other musicians whether they are French or English. In any case, it will surely help to know what the C stands for when they suggest we play the Bach Prelude in C, and not in Sea.

Purring

How big a world should I live in? Knowing that I am free to travel around the planet is such a privilege. For most people it is a necessity to be able to say "been there, done that". This is what motivated my youthful urges for discovery. Later, work assignments sent me away and broadened my perspective. Everywhere I went, I was fascinated to notice that happiness is possible in so many different ways everywhere and for everyone.

Being proudly supportive of our local sports teams make us wave flags and brag about our superiority. Of course our quest for survival requires some combative spirit. Interviewing for work the first time, is always an awakening to the ground rule of employers: selecting only the best fit for the job. Once you are in, you realize you need to master a new set of rules. Employers each have their own performance appraisal process. Understanding how to please your supervisor becomes essential to get a salary increase. Blending in some audacity will get you spotted by higher echelons and possibly move you up the ladder. So you hold on to your rung and avoid having your fingers crunched by whoever is stepping on the levels above. Then one day, you make it to the top. The unobstructed view from up there is quite impressive. Pride and honours fill your ego but stress keeps you on your toes. Soon you realize how narrow and slippery the top of the pyramid becomes. The only way from there is down, but you smartly manage your parachute for a soft landing.

Eventually you notice that being grounded can be just as rewarding. Other smart people around you live outside of the rat race and look much happier and healthier for it. Not being on the move as much lets you set roots in your preferred environment. Stronger anchorage increases your chances of survival in storms and gives you time to appreciate people and things around you. Otherwise, you may only be drifting over them, on your way somewhere else. Just like a happy neighborhood cat, I would much rather busy myself at establishing my own safe and fun territory. So don't be surprised to hear me purring next to a cat on my favourite patio chair.

Migrant Credit or Debit

Canada and other rich countries of the world must adopt a way to manage the unprecedented surge of migrants. Wars or natural disasters have encouraged millions of people to flee their country. Internet and television have shown them how life is good elsewhere and one day, they show up at our border.

All humans are born equal, in theory at least. Soon enough, a child realizes where home is located on this planet. Some, luckier than others, are in for an easy ride, right from the start. But when home is unsafe, migrating becomes the number one priority. Most of our own ancestors saved us the work and migrated in the past so, why can't migrants do it today?

Countries are challenged to house and feed newcomers in need. What if the solution came from a worldwide consensus instituted at all levels of government. A 1% credit or debit would help fund migrants settlements. United Nations would initiate the process by debiting each country an extra 1% of their annual fee, refundable by a 1% credit if this country accepted at least 1% of the world migrating population each year. The extras if any would be distributed at pro-rata to hosting countries.

Canada has always been a popular destination and should not have any problem getting a credit form the UN. Much more funding would be needed and would come from the same ruling imposed on all levels of government, provincial and municipal. Cities would do the same through municipal taxation. A 1% additional amount would be added for the migrant support program. This amount could be credited when a letter from the town citizens' association would confirm that a citizen has donated at least ten hours of volunteer work helping migrants. Each town could use the funds collected to pay rent and food until migrants could earn a salary from work. Parents would be invited to attend school with their children to learn the language, help the teachers and blend-in with locals faster. Local businesses could also avoid this new tax by employing migrants. This way the whole country would have a shoulder to the wheel that soon would start rolling along smoothly and peacefully.

Sources

When visibility counts and it often does, using the internet can make you be quickly seen and heard all over the world. And the beauty of it is that it can be done at minimal cost. But many hours and loads of determination later, your message can go viral and have millions of followers.

A catchy topic is the key. If you have a good hook in the beginning and can keep the attention of the reader for at least a minute, you may have a winner. Like a giant wheel, it will take enormous effort to get it moving and up to your desired speed. But once there, momentum will be your ally in having it remain popular as long as you give it a daily push.

Sara had now made it to that point. Like the past five generations of her ancestors, she lives in Sources, a small town with a population of 2,000 in Newfoundland. The majority of her school friends had left to live somewhere else in larger cities of the world. But some had come back, convinced that nowhere else gave them such a sense of belonging as

Sources did. Nestled in a broad bay facing Labrador, the sunset on Sources is spectacular. Dozens of boats are moored in this deep bay facing west. They look as if they are resting in a safe haven, protected from the east winds, howling over 'The Rock' after crossing the raging Atlantic.

Knowing she would not find any other place she would enjoy living in as much, Sara was determined to work her way out of welfare, in Sources. Qualified to be a high-school teacher, she was deeply dismayed that job openings may not be available for another ten years, when the present teachers may retire. Her meagre income was made as an occasional teacher, rarely for more than a month. A lot of other residents were dependent on welfare, and she could see the harmful effects of it on their pride. Writing had always been a passion for Sara and, combined with her good looks, social media quickly connected her to thousands of other word enthusiasts around the world.

Sara followed the advice of other published authors and managed to have her first novel published. She was invited by librarians to present her book all over Newfoundland. And then one day it happened, the book went viral. London, Paris and New York wanted to see her. Did she go? Not for long because she was always glad to return and drop anchor in Sources.

Savannah

From his hotel room window, watching the sunrise over Savannah, GA, Henry could not help reminiscing on how much of a close call it had been. Susan and Henry had visited this lovely town about fifteen years ago. They were only stopping by for a few hours but got a good enough taste of it to anxiously want to come back. Every few streets of the historic district have a small central place set with benches under giant centuries-old oak trees. Most of them were planned in 1733 by General James Oglethorpe to keep cattle and vegetable gardens close to each residential district of the town. He called them wards and 22 of them still exist today. They are now many oases with shady benches that show up every six streets as you walk through the historic district. Many harbour a monument or a fountain honoring a patriot that helped create or fought to save this jewel of the South.

Tourists have to slow-down and relax in order to fit the easygoing way of the locals. It takes a few days to grasp every word as they round them up melodiously. Henry noticed that Susan was starting to blend-in but he was surprised when she said the same about his new southern drawl. Their hotel was located in the historic district and the concierge gave them a map highlighting top rated restaurants and sites. A trolley tour was booked for the next two days with up-on and off privileges. They were the first to get on the bus and preferred to sit in the back section that had fully opened sides without windows. The weather was a perfect 65°F with bright sunshine and light wind.

Julia was the driver and she welcomed everybody by asking each of the thirty passengers where they were from. All were Americans from all over the USA even as far as Hawaii. In her mid-fifties, Julia had been driving this tour bus for twelve years and said she loved every day of it. Meeting happy people coming from all over the world ready to enjoy her hometown kept her joyful. She manoeuvred her bus with military sharpness around narrow streets and corners, barely inches away from parked cars. The last part of the tour is on the river front. To get there she had to drive down the steep incline of a narrow alley covered with cobblestones. As she was showing them the many Factors' Walks over the side alley, the brakes of the trolley stopped working. She yelled "hold-on" and had only seconds to downshift and use the engine to slow us down. The Riverfront Street below and boardwalk were full of people. Julia blew the trolley horn to signal the danger while she steered between two pedestrians crossing the street. The trolley turned but almost capsized as the wheels on the right side went up in the air. Passengers helped to balance the bus by all leaning the on the lifted side and landed it back. Julia, who had kept her cool, announced with a broad smile, that this was The Cotton Exchange Tavern planned stop and all drinks were on her.

Epilogue

Hopefully you have enjoyed reading my stories as much as I find it salutary for me writing them. Beauty is everywhere around us and needs only a little help to get our attention. I feel like I am on a mission to let the Good be on top of the news for a change like I did in the story 'Sorrow Bin' for which Ray Allison wrote: « I like your positive attitude to life, full of resolve to make it better ». She is part of my writing group along with: Gail Campbell, Stella Charleson, Margaret Meagher, Val Campbell and Shirley Skilling. I will forever be grateful for the support and critiques of such gifted writers.

Driven by the recent discovery of the pleasure of writing, every morning at breakfast I let my imagination carry me where it pleases. I never thought it was possible. Such freedom of mind is available to all as long as you are lucky enough to live where freedom of thought is allowed.

This passion is addictive but so useful for massaging the intellect and repelling senility that I wish it for all.

Alphabetical List of Stories

Alphabetical List of Stories

My Gratitude for Critiques and Support goes to:

Sylvie Lussier
Andrée Duchesneau
Jonathan Brunet
Ralph & Ray Allison
Margaret Meagher
Val Campbell
Stella Charleson
Gail Campbell
Shirley Skilling
Pat & Nancy Matronianos
Pam Parsons
Bob Hazlett.

Made in the USA
Columbia, SC
25 February 2019